I0769713

"Run, Rabbit, Run"
© 2024 by Juniper Hartmann

All rights reserved. No part of this publication may be reproduced, distributed, or transmitted in any form or by any means, including photocopying, recording, or other electronic or mechanical methods, without the prior written permission of the publisher, except in the case of brief quotations embodied in critical reviews and certain other noncommercial uses permitted by copyright law. For permission requests, write to the publisher, addressed "Attention: Permissions Coordinator," at the e-mail address below.

Email: Hello@JuniperHartmann.com
Website: JuniperHartmann.com

ISBN (paperback): 979-8-9911323-8-1
ISBN (e-book): 979-8-9911323-1-2

Cover Designer: The Red Fox Creative
Interior Designer: The Red Fox Creative
Editor: Lillith Haven

RUN, RABBIT, RUN

JUNIPER HARTMANN

FOR MYSELF,
FIRST AND
FOREMOST.

AND FOR YOU,
IF YOU'RE INTO
THAT SORT
OF THING.

Author's Note

FROM JUNIE

It has become apparent to me that the dark romance genre is missing a crucial component: educational content related to the BDSM lifestyle.

To that end, I have included an afterward to provide better context and help newcomers engage safely with their darkest fantasies… should they choose to do so.

It's important to know that you do not have to engage with your desires outside of fantasies. For some, their imagination and favorite toy are enough. Sometimes the thought of something is better than the act.

Please Read This
TRIGGER WARNINGS

There are quite a few trigger warnings in this book. Please understand that it's impossible to predict all the triggers present in the audience and this is not a complete list of possibly upsetting themes.

If any of these are dealbreakers, I highly suggest you do not continue reading:

- *Sexual Assault*
- *Physical Assault*
- *Humilation / Degradation*
- *Group Sex (MMFM)*
- *Forced Exhibitionism*
- *Forced Orgasms*

Chapter One

The forest was hauntingly still outside of her frantic panting. Everything seemed hopeless, but Bunny had to believe. The thrashing heart in her chest set a steady beat to which she moved her aching limbs.

Just get to the clearing… get to the clearing… You can do this, Bunny. She soothed herself with words she knew fell empty. Bunny's only hope for escape lay beyond the treeline, which was two miles out according to her captor. It was a distance she cleared easily during her early morning runs.

However, that was at a relaxed pace on flat, even pavement, courtesy of her secluded suburb. Currently, she was carelessly crashing through overgrowth over winter-hardened ground, desperately trying to outrun the danger.

The situation served to cement her long-held belief that nature wanted you dead. The weak perished immediately. The strong lasted longer but died all the same in the end. And what was she? The weak, or the strong? As of yet, Bunny couldn't determine the answer.

The cold air ripped at her raw throat as she sucked in frigid lungfuls. Trees crowded her on all sides, with their thick, looming boughs blocking all moonlight.

Although her eyes had adjusted to the velvet dark, she felt no relief from the fear. It would almost be better if she were still blindfolded. At least then she wouldn't have to face the danger closing in, the hungry wolf nipping at her heels.

If she stopped, he'd swallow her whole.

The thought spurred her faster, mind spinning with the possibilities of how he might decide to use her body. Before setting her loose into the woods, her captor had made clear that she was no longer her own person if he caught her. Instead, she was a possession—something to be used however he saw fit.

Abruptly, Bunny felt herself pitching forward, tumbling to the ground with a shock that took her breath away.

She paused, her breath held tight in her chest, taking stock of her body, still numb with adrenaline. Her arms were raw from the impact with the frozen ground, since she had instinctively thrown them out to protect her face. Thankfully, they weren't too badly damaged. Even so, the building pain proved the ground was still unrelenting in its rigidity even as the warmth of spring was budding.

This was proven further by her feet, which had gone numb after what must have been over a mile. Her sneakers were crusted in spring-time mud, which was also splattered up her legs.

On the bright side, it meant she didn't have far to go, should her internal compass serve her right. And, with burgeoning hope in her heart, Bunny realized she hadn't seen a trace of her kidnapper yet.

But realistically, that thought brought little comfort. He was sure to know these woods while she didn't know them at all, and Bunny had the creeping suspicion he was toying with her. These were his hunting grounds, after all. From what she knew of sadists, half the fun would be raising her hope just to watch it drain.

As if on command, she heard dry twigs snapping from behind her, and something inside of her snapped, as well, as panic shot through her. "Oh, my poor Bunny," A deep voice crooned, "I do hope you didn't hurt yourself. Damaging my property is a punishable offense."

Fuck, fuck, oh fuck, she thought, tears pricking at her eyes, cold on her face.

Bunny whipped her head around, sending auburn hair flying in limp, sweaty strands, desperately gauging his distance from her.

"I'll give you one more chance, Bunny, and a thirty-second head start. You're very close. I'm impressed, honestly." There was humor in his voice, and it turned her stomach. This was nothing but a game to him. For her, it was likely life or death... or a fate far worse.

Bunny scrambled to her feet, catching herself from falling again when her stiff legs gave way. Once she had her bearings, she took off, dashing madly. It couldn't be more than a half mile to the finish line.

Her captor had told her there was a break in the trees only two miles out from where he had let her go. She could go free if she made it there before he caught her. If not...

The thought made her tears flow freely.

She wore the smile of a person who couldn't believe their fate as they were led to the gallows, a hysterical grin that made her breath come out in waves of steam rather than puffs.

Finally, salvation could be seen through a clear patch of sky in the distance: a thinning of trees, where moonlight touched the earth. It was the push she needed to run harder, even as everything around her stilled to slow motion.

And then, something was wrapped around her midsection.

An arm. His arm.

"Gotcha."

His voice dripped with glee. It made Bunny feel sick. She twisted, pushing hard against his steely hold on her, to try and ram her head into his face.

The headbutt landed, and the shock loosened her captor's grip. Bunny pushed away, turned on heel, and shot forward. Her eyes were alight with fear and quickly fading hope as she desperately careened toward the clearing.

But then she felt herself in free fall, landing with a crushing weight pressing her into the hardened earth. Pain exploded through her already aching body.

"Oh, my poor, frightened, Bunny," His breath warmed her ear as he panted from the exertion, but she shuddered even as the chill of the night faded, "I would say you don't have anything to fear... but after that stunt, I think that would be a lie."

Bunny struggled, but it wasn't any use. His weight kept her spent body pinned, and she was losing her will to fight back. Why bother? She didn't think it even mattered anymore.

He pulled back, keeping her back flush with his chest, her legs dragging against the ground until they were both on their knees.

"You need to behave before you make things worse for yourself," Her captor hissed, grabbing her chin with one hand while gathering her wrists with the other. Bunny froze, holding her breath as terror bloomed in full.

Once she stilled, her captor kissed her temple and whispered, "Good girl." The tender gesture made her yank away, earning a quiet laugh from the sociopath holding her.

He released her chin, moving his hand. She could hear the distinctive clink of metal, and her heart plummeted.

Before Bunny could work up the will to fight for freedom again, he had snapped a handcuff around one of her wrists and held the other in an iron grip.

She began thrashing, knowing it wouldn't help a thing. Instead of loosening his grip, Bunny's struggle only served to dig the metal cuff painfully into her wrist. Her captor calmly slapped the other cuff and closed it securely.

"There we are," He murmured, holding one of her forearms and stroking it with his thumb, "It won't hurt unless you struggle... and that would be stupid, Bunny. There's no point in hurting yourself, especially when you're about to receive your first punishment. It'll hurt enough on its own, I promise you that."

"Punishment" struck her like lightning, and horror exploded in its wake, radiating through her quivering limbs.

She heard him stand. Her heart hammered. From the corner of her eye, Bunny saw black combat boots. His breathing was slightly labored, evidence that he had exerted at least some energy during the chase. While it was fleeting, she did felt at least a little satisfaction from this revelation.

With a soft sound, her captor lowered himself to the ground and reached over to her. Grabbing one of her arms, he kept his other hand firmly on her side and slid her over to him.

She ended up draped over his lap.

"What are you going to do to me?" She whispered frantically, voice breaking.

Her captor gripped her chin, turning her head to face him.

"You are not to speak unless spoken to, little Bunny. While you're learning, I have something that will help you remember." His voice was soft. In a different situation, she might have even called it soothing.

His backpack rustled as he reached into it, and soon he was holding a ball gag to her mouth expectantly.

"You're insa-" She started, but the words were halted as he shoved the ball into her mouth and pulled the straps tight around her head. Her eyes widened and Bunny began to flail once more, whipping her head around and thrusting her tongue in a futile effort to dislodge the silicone ball.

"Sure am, but that seems like even more reason to follow the rules and be a good girl," He responded briskly, fastening the gag with little difficulty, "Are you ready to learn why you should behave for me?"

The tide of his voice had turned harsh, and the waves crashed hard on her already fraying nerves. She was terrified of his wrath.

Her captor began pulling her leggings down, just until her ass was bared to the cold night air. Goosebumps pricked across her skin.

"Normally I would make you count, but since you can't seem to control your mouth, I'll let it slide this time."

Bunny began screaming through the gag. It wasn't a noise formed from fear, however. There was a powerless fury burning hot in her now. Not that it would matter; this location was remote. Her captor had taken her somewhere he could be sure she wouldn't be heard.

Bunny felt him shift a leg, sliding it over the back of her knees, restraining them. He raised his hand and slammed down, flicking his wrist right before making contact. Bunny cried out in pain, tears pricking as her ass began to sharply smart.

The blows continued until she was whimpering and choking on her sobs around the ball gag. Every impact rang out like a gunshot in the quiet around them.

She whimpered, forehead pressed into the dirt. The humiliation was the worst part. Her cheeks, both sets, burned bright; one with shame, the other with pain.

"Enough of that, my Bunny," Her captor said softly once it was over, reaching to gently cup her chin, his thumb stroking her cheek. "Running from me never works. You'll learn that well."

There was more rustling, and then the clink of a bottle.

"I don't want to struggle with you. This will make things easier on the both of us."

Bunny turned her head to watch him pull liquid into a needle from a small vial. Then, she screamed, the sound ringing out ragged and despondent in the calm of the forest.

Then a prick.
Then darkness.

19

Chapter Two

Bunny was encased in a soft warmth she never wanted to part with. It felt like she was lying weightless in the clouds. But it also felt like she had a head full of cotton, her mouth dry enough for her tongue to stick to her top palette.

She slowly shifted in the gentle embrace of whatever she was wrapped up in. Her eyes fluttered slowly and she lifted her head an inch or so above the pillow. And then the horror came flooding back. With a racing heart, she froze.

That is, until Bunny realized that she was also completely naked, save for a thick collar that was fastened around her neck. It wasn't uncomfortable physically, but mentally it threw her into a frenzy. She reached up in a panic to rip it off and found that it was secured with a lock.

Okay, just relax. Chill out. You're going to get through this. It's just a collar. It's not going to kill you, Bunny thought to herself.

Her eyes began adjusting to the low light. What she saw gave her a change of heart: instead of freezing in place, the organ now plummeted like a weight into her lower stomach.

The walls around her were filled with sex toys of every sort. There were recessed walls with shelving and drawers lining them to the midpoint, hooks hanging with whips and other implements above them.

Around the room, an array of wicked machines and imposing restraint systems stood like wardens.

"Hello, sweet Bunny," A voice, gentle as silk, sounded through the silence.

Bunny realized she had been holding her breath as soon as she gasped. Her head whipped around, and she immediately recognized the movement as a mistake as the soft pounding turned to a roar of pain. Her hands flew up to cradle her head.

"Careful now, my Bunny," The man murmured, drawing closer, "You're going to need a few hours to get back to normal. Haldol and Ativan are a hell of a combination. Extremely effective at sedation, but there are drawbacks."

Bunny opened her mouth in response but found her voice faltering. It felt like her mind was stuck in place, a record scratching, desperately trying to gain traction.

How could this happen to her?

Just a few weeks ago, she had been celebrating her upcoming graduation from college. She had been accepted to her first choice university for graduate school. Her life was good.

This isn't fair… She thought, tears welling up before she had time to stop them. Large, fat drops began to run down her face as her chest tightened like a fist.

A coldness settled over her that not even the plush blanket wrapped around her body could stave. She was as good as dead, wasn't she?

No, she thought fiercely, *You can't think like that. Others have gotten out of similar situations. You can do this. Just concentrate, cooperate, and wait.*

Her captor had been watching passively until she began to cry, then he clucked his tongue and shook his head. "Now, now, Bunny, enough of that, or I'll give you something to cry about." There was a vein of amusement in his voice.

He's mocking me, she realized with bristling fury, *How fucking dare he?*

"I'm sorry, sir, I just can't help but think my parents must be so worried," She whispered, looking up at him through her eyelashes in a submissive gesture.

His face immediately darkened.

"Do you think I'm stupid?" He asked softly, but she could feel anger lurking under the surface of his words.

"I- I'm sorry?" she stammered, confusion in her shrill voice.

"You heard me. Answer the question." He was now stalking toward her, gleaming leather loafers padding softly on the wooden floor.

"N-no! Of course, I don't. I'm so sorry. I just… I wanted to explain why I was crying." Bunny was now scrambling backward, trying to keep herself covered while replacing the distance his long legs were quickly eating.

Her captor stopped at the edge of the pad she was lying on. It was large, easily the size of an area rug, and thick enough to protect her from the wooden floor beneath.

"Then don't try to play me. Your old life is gone, Bunny. This is your reality now," Her captor said evenly, eyes boring holes into the top of her bowed head, "I promise it isn't as bad as you think it is. There are far worse men out there who take women to torture them for gratification. I'm not like that."

She sniffled, still softly crying in the hopeless way only a broken person can.

"Understand that if you follow the rules, you'll be fine. I will punish you if you misbehave.

Your pain doesn't necessarily bring me pleasure, but I will cause you pain all the same."

As his voice faded, leaving a hollow silence interrupted only by her hiccuping sobs, Bunny felt herself crumple to the ground once more.

She had absolutely been trying to "play" him, after all. The first rule of survival was to humanize yourself to your kidnapper, or so the crime shows would have her believe.

"Why are you doing this? Why won't you just let me go? I won't tell anybody. I swear I won't." She whimpered softly.

"Because I want to." He answered simply, "And it had to happen to somebody. Would you like to pick somebody to trade places with?"

Fury flashed through her chest, and she snapped her head to look him in the eyes.

"Actually yeah. I would. I can go ahead and name a few people I wouldn't have any sympathy for in my position. Why? Are you offering to kidnap one of them instead?" She hissed, baring her teeth. Flashbacks to mean girls and bullies flitted through her mind, the objects of her ire through her younger years.

Bunny wasn't sure where this feeling of bold defiance had come from, but the release of anger felt cathartic. It was like she was gaining ground in some way.

Her captor's eyes darkened, and she began to suspect she had made a mistake.

"What a bitter bitch," Even though his voice was still low, it had deepened significantly, "Wishing this upon a person is insane. "

Before her better judgment could stop her, Bunny's eyes bugged out of her head, and she let loose a bitter laugh. His eyebrow raised.

"Are you fucking serious? I'm insane? Me? You have me locked in a bedroom doubling as a sex dungeon after hunting me through the goddamn woods like an animal, and now you're sitting there saying my desire for revenge against people who have actually done wrong by me is-" She stopped short as he stepped forward, closing the distance between them.

Her captor knelt, head lowering to look down at her as she sat, trembling with fear.

"I'm warning you, Bunny. I love a woman with a little fire in her blood… But I'm only going to put up with so much before I put you in your place."

Bunny snapped her mouth shut with no intention of taking it any further. So much for gaining his sympathy.

The scent of cedar and smoke wafted off of him, and she imagined it was his cologne, spritzed lightly on the crisp black sweater he wore. The aroma was enticing, like something that called you home. She shifted uncomfortably.

His forearms rested on his knees, large hands clasped as he stared steadily at her. His deep, dark eyes were unreadable.

"I'm sorry," She whispered through free-flowing tears, "I'm so sorry…" But it wasn't just her captor she was speaking to.

She was sorry for so much more than that.

"May I ask something?" She whispered, eyes focused on the floor.

"Of course, Bunny. Just mind your manners." He responded, sounding amused.

"Why did you choose me? Was it my looks?" The question had been nagging at her since the first moment she realized she was being kidnapped. Bunny had always been beautiful, often aware of the favors it earned her. Her captor let out a barking laugh.

"That's quite the assumption, Bunny," He murmured, reaching out to cup her chin in his hand. She stiffened but thought better of pulling away. "How incredibly vain."

He stroked her cheek gently with his thumb, humming thoughtfully to himself. But he didn't answer the question.

Suddenly, her captor released her and stood up, striding toward the door. After opening it, he turned around to look at her one last time.

"I'll be back in a few hours, little Bunny. There's food and water beside your bed. You should recoup your strength before our first training session, especially after our playtime in the woods."

She could have vomited at his usage of the word, "playtime." It was clear that's all this was to him: a game. She was unlucky enough to be both his opponent and his prize.

With that, he slipped out of the door. Bunny glanced over, noticing a box with water bottles and single-serving packages of snacks. But she couldn't possibly eat. She didn't have the energy to do anything, and her stomach was turning as it was.

Instead, Bunny curled into a ball on the soft padding, pulled the blanket around her, buried her face in the pillow, and cried.

Chapter Three

The past always seemed to catch up with Bunny, whether she was holding it close to her chest like a security blanket, or at an arm's length in desperation to make it *go away*.

Pain is funny in that eventually you begin to find familiarity in it, and with that new normal comes comfort. You become all too content with the drowning weight of sadness.

Her suffering felt all-consuming, the darkness of her past ever-looming.

While Bunny could feel the fierce pangs in her belly, she couldn't bring herself to touch any of the food her captor had left. She knew it would taste like ash in her mouth. Instead, she plucked a water bottle from the basket and twisted the top off with shaking fingers.

Bunny's dark green manicure was chipping. Not that it mattered much. Who did she have to impress? Certainly not the sociopath who had kidnapped her.

A vortex of dark thoughts spun in her pounding head regardless of the haze: hand-covered ears picking up the distant shouting of an angry man as he ripped a door open and slammed it closed. Not to leave the room, no. Just to hear the noise and feel catharsis in the violence of the act.

The physical conflicts had happened far more often than Bunny cared to remember. Half of the time she couldn't, anyway. She had always been her father's child, high on temper and low on self-control during her episodic anger.

Her mother was the opposite. That demure woman never stood a chance against the wrath Bunny's father rained on his household whenever he lost his temper. But honestly, Bunny had a hard time finding sympathy. Her mother should have protected her as a child. She hadn't.

With a start, Bunny realized she had been spiraling, deep in her thoughts. Lately, she had these thoughts more and more. Her therapist called them emotional flashbacks.

Even when she was doing nothing related to any of it. Even when she was trying to do anything but think about what life was like before she managed to escape and build something better for herself.

Maybe the social workers who got involved were right. Perhaps this situation was exactly what she should have expected from herself, what she deserved. Girls from broken homes made stupid mistakes, and those oversights landed them in places like this.

She had read the reports compiled by the people who had come to investigate the bruises left on her when her father lost control. Her purported fate had been repeated over and over by stiff professionals who were clear about their lack of faith in her future because of her past.

Bunny had always said she would never be a statistic… But at the end of the day, she knew everybody was a statistic, a sum of their demographics.

What the fuck is this and why does it have to happen to me? Was all she could think. Her head still felt like it was full of cotton, the haze continuing even now, hours later.

Bunny was only familiar with Ativan. She'd been given Benzos by her psychiatrist when the panic attacks began growing more intense. The other drug mentioned was foreign to her.

Bunny wanted to cry again, but tears were nowhere to be found. Separation from self was simply a way of life when you grew up with heavy trauma, and only bad ways out.

Depersonalization became your daily reality. It felt like a waking nightmare. Or so she had thought. No, Bunny was quickly realizing that the true nightmare was the horrifying situation she had found herself thrust into.

This wasn't supposed to happen. She had fought, clawed, and tore through the academic world to obtain a full-ride scholarship. She busted and hauled ass to get where she was.

And next? Graduate school, where she would gain a Masters in Archeology, to be followed by a Doctorate. She had bled for this life and had made things happen that she only halfway thought were possible.

And now, it was seemingly all for nothing.

Bunny took a few tentative sips of the water, grateful it was room temperature. She doubted her stomach could handle the shock of cold liquid. Setting aside the bottle, Bunny laid back down and fell into the hazy catatonia she had found so much comfort in during the worst of her younger years.

With any luck, it would get her through this hellish situation, too.

A hand rapping at the door startled

Bunny. Is he seriously knocking? She thought, bewildered by the bizarre decision.

Her captor had taken her dignity. Why the hell would he give her the illusion of privacy?

In the next moment, a new person entered the room. He was dressed similarly to her captor; understated but expensive. Bunny wheeled backward, curling her knees to her chest and crossing her feet, arms wrapped over her breasts.

"Hello, Barbara. My name is Michael. I'm Demetrius' assistant." The man said pleasantly, as though he were meeting an acquaintance and not standing in front of a naked, kidnapped girl.

He had tousled brown hair, black glasses with a square frame, and a five-o'clock shadow. Bunny immediately had the feeling that he was one of those people who always seemed unkempt, regardless of the effort put into his appearance.

The word she was trying to conjure wasn't sleazy, but sleazy was close enough.

Bunny gulped, cheeks heating at her exposure, before looking at him, pleading clear in her expression. "Please, Michael, you have to help me. Demetrius kidnapped me. This isn't by choice, and I need your help. My friends and family will be incredibly worried. Please." Her voice was hushed and pleading. She didn't actually have many friends, and her family didn't give a shit, but he didn't have to know that.

"You can walk around this basement apartment as much as you want tomorrow. Demetrius wants to begin working with you before then, though. There's a kitchen down the hall with anything you need in it… except for sharp objects, of course." He chuckled at the end of his own sentence and her jaw almost dropped. He was in on it.

"What the fuck is wrong with you people?" She screeched.

"For what it's worth, I sympathize with your position, Barbara... But it's kind of out of my hands. And it's not all bad, I promise. Demetrius isn't a bad man-" Michael was cut off by incredulous laughter.

"Are you out of your fucking mind? Not a bad man? He kidnapped me, chased me through the woods, assaulted me, and now he's keeping me here against my will. He's a goddamn monster, and you are too if you don't help me get the fuck out of here." By the end, she was shrieking and trembling with anger.

"I'm sorry, Barbara, but I can't help you." He snapped as though agitated with her.

With that, Michael turned and left the room, and Bunny screamed after him, "And don't call me Barbara, asshole! My name is BUNNY."

Frankly, she felt a little ridiculous. People often questioned her nickname. What self-respecting adult insisted people call them a cutesy name for a rabbit?

But the nickname was hers. She chose it, and a title felt immeasurably important compared to what little she *could* choose about herself.

Even so, it did feel silly to be screaming at an accomplice to her kidnapping and assault, demanding he call her "Bunny."

Just then, she realized that Michael had used a name: Demetrius. Bunny now knew who had done this to her. *What a stupid name,* she thought as she crossed her arms.

Another knock sounded soon after Michael left. This time, it was loud and confident instead of loose and timid. She knew it was Demetrius before he opened the door.

Bunny looked away, fear pooling in her belly and tightening her dry throat. She wanted more water but was frozen as she waited for him to make the first move.

"Hello, little Bunny." He purred, stalking forward like a panther. He was sleek, attractive, and predatory in all the right ways. His black hair and dark eyes created a stunning picture. In a different situation, she might have pined after him. In the current circumstances, Bunny wanted nothing more than to drive a knife through his bastard neck.

"It's Barbara to you, you fucking sicko. What do you want?" She was nearly squeaking as her pulse picked up, racing faster the closer he came. It was a wonder she could find the courage to be so disrespectful… but fuck him, honestly.

She might take issue with anybody else using the formal version of her name. But this deranged lunatic? It was the only name she wanted in his mouth. Her nickname made it feel like he had claimed some intimacy with her that he had no right to.

"I just want to check in on you. I gave you a hefty dose and that comes with side effects." He grabbed a chair without slowing down and dragged it with him as he approached her.

Demetrius swung the chair around in one movement and sat in it, looking every bit like a bored monarch giving council to his lowly serf.

She wanted to ask for clarification on the cocktail of drugs, but she decided she'd rather not know the specifics. Instead, Bunny swallowed, attempting to wet her throat, and decided to play along. That was the right decision, wasn't it? To keep your captor placated and happy until help arrived?

She hoped to God it was because she'd be

pissed if she ended up on one of those late-night True Crime shows as a cautionary tale.

Don't be a dumb bitch, or you'll end up like this dumb bitch, she thought sardonically.

"I'm fine. Thank you for the water," Was all she could manage.

"Good, I'm glad," He rested his elbow on the arm of the chair, leaning slightly to rest his face in his hand, "Now, come here. Crawl to me."

Bunny froze, eyes widening as she waited to see if this asshole was serious.

From the look of it, he was.

"You can make this easy or hard on yourself, Bunny. I won't repeat myself and you have five seconds to comply. One, two, three…" He started counting, and Bunny eased herself to her knees until she was exactly where she didn't want to be: right where he wanted her.

She was all too aware of her nakedness. Blame it on the rise of contrived perfection via social media or the constant weight of societal expectations placed on the shoulders of women, but she had never been comfortable in her skin. Even though she knew she was stunningly attractive, she struggled with self-esteem.

Bunny trained her eyes on the floor as she shifted, chewing her lower lip.

Once she was on all fours at his feet,

she felt a hand slip under her chin and jerked back, sucking a quick breath through her nose. Demetrius simply chuckled and then grabbed her chin more firmly.

"So jumpy, little Bunny. But I do love seeing you like this, so helpless and fragile." When she glanced up, her eyes meeting his, he looked amused.

The *fucker*.

"What do you say we get acquainted? I'll start. My name is Demetrius. I'm an entrepreneur with a few projects in the works. I spend most of my limited free time reading and working on myself."

He sounded like a douchebag. Of course, he'd refer to himself as an entrepreneur, and of course, he would feel it necessary to mention that… as though it was relevant in any capacity. He needed everybody to know that he was his own boss.

"Your turn." He said, tightening his grip on her chin.

She gritted her teeth, "My name's Bunny and I'm a student. I like margaritas and long walks on the beach…. Oh, and mentally stable men who don't kidnap and assault me." She returned the casual tone with a little more flair, mocking his ridiculous introduction.

"Oh, good. It's nice to see you still have a sense of humor under all that fear." He chuckled, stroking the side of her jaw with his thumb.

She recoiled again at the tender gesture. Demetrius shot his hand out and grabbed her by the neck. Bunny froze as the crush of his grip began to restrict her breathing.

"What do you say we start in full, Bunny? You seem like you're feeling up to it. I'm ready to play if you are." He said with an enthusiasm that made her skin crawl.

Bunny's heart plummeted to her stomach and then shot up into her throat, the sensation making her nauseous. She was most certainly not ready and never would be. But it was obvious this man was not used to hearing the word, "No." She briefly wondered if he was even aware of its existence.

"I really wish you'd just let me go." She whimpered, looking up at him through tear-beaded eyelashes.

"I can't do that for you, Bunny. But I can do other things I know you'll like if you learn to relax into the pleasure I'm about to bring you."

Chapter Four

Demetrius rolled his sleeves up, revealing muscular forearms. He didn't take his eyes off her the entire time.

Those dark eyes raked slowly down her body from head to toe, drinking in everything the slender woman had to offer. She had always been slight in stature, often one of the smallest people in the room. Her pillowy breasts were half-hidden by flowing red hair falling in layers, but even so, it was obvious that they were pert and perky.

A deep flush had grown from her cheeks down into her chest. She wasn't sure what this sociopath had planned for her but she was certain it wasn't going to be pleasant. For her, at least.

Demetrius walked over to the seating arranged meticulously around the grand fireplace built into the wall between the array of toys decorating the rest of the space to either side. The seating area became the focal point for

Bunny even despite the sexual apparatuses that had caught her attention so readily before.

She also noticed a large four-poster bed placed dead in the center of the room she had somehow missed while struggling through the aftereffects of what he had drugged her with.

Demetrius made his way over to the couch. "Come here, Bunny." His voice was firm and commanding. She was frozen for a few heartbeats before noticing his narrowed eyes, a clear warning that more transgressions would bring more punishments.

She stood up and slowly began walking, until his voice stopped her dead in her tracks.

"Crawl."

A rising anger began building within her. Was it not enough that he was about to thoroughly violate her? Did he need to humiliate her, as well? Even so, she did as she was bidden, and sank to her knees. Crawling slowly toward him, Bunny kept her eyes trained on the floor, eyes raw from her constant crying.

Her current tears were not formed from sadness. No, she was angry. She could feel the same rage roaring that had gotten her into trouble before. Bunny wasn't usually physically violent, though, unlike her father. She preferred to exercise her grievances through more conniving means, and she was no stranger to social subversion when she felt wronged.

Without that avenue of release for her rage, she was beginning to think that violence of a more tangible form would be her only option.

Once Bunny thought she was close enough to please him, she stilled, trembling.

"Oh, my sweet Bunny. So fearful," Demetrius murmured, reaching down to softly hold her chin between his thumb and pointer fingers, "You don't have to be afraid. I know this isn't something you want right now… But you will want it. I promise. I don't want this to be bad for you."

Bunny's face twisted into a snarl, her blue-green eyes rising to meet his. "I'm not scared," She hissed, "I'm pissed." His eyebrows shot up at her outburst. And then a sinister smile slowly spread until his bright white teeth were fully bared in a lupine grin.

"Oh, you'll be fun to break, won't you?"

Fun wasn't the word that came to her mind, but if the bastard wanted to keep that outlook, he was welcome to it.

Demetrius released her and turned slightly to open a black box next to him that she hadn't noticed before from her position on the floor. She couldn't see its contents, perhaps blessedly so. When he turned back, he was holding a small bottle of lube and a moderately sized butt plug.

"Lay yourself across my lap." He said, black eyes burning into hers. The intensity was enough to make her shift nervously, the flush deepening. Even as her brain screamed to run, her body obeyed him, fearing the consequences a refusal would bring. Gingerly, she crawled onto the couch and draped herself over his legs.

"Good girl," He said, reaching to stroke her face with the back of his pointer finger, "Tell me, have you ever had your ass filled?"

Bunny gulped, fighting the almost irresistible urge to rip her face from his hand and shy away. "I have, yes." The response was short and strained. Much to her chagrin, she could feel her body responding to the idea of anal play. It was one of her favorite bedroom activities, and she could feel warmth building between her legs.

Briefly, Bunny wondered if he was right. Did she want this? Her fantasies had centered around situations like her current one since she was young. That much was true. But the difference was consent. If she engaged in non-consensual play, it was always accompanied by a safeword and an understanding of her autonomy. Here, in this hell, there were no safe words.

"Good. Then this won't come as a shock,"

With that, he laid the plug on the small of her back and poured lube onto one of his hands.

Demetrius' fingers slipped between her plump ass cheeks and he gently prodded the tight entrance between them. Bunny whimpered before she could stop herself, then gritted her teeth. The bastard chuckled in response before slipping a finger inside. She knew her face was bright red, but she refused to give him the satisfaction of admitting to her conflicted feelings.

Demetrius began working another finger in, twisting and scissoring them to ready her body for the plug. She wriggled at the attention, eyes squeezed shut against the pleasurable feeling building in her belly.

"That's it, good girl. Relax into it." He murmured, continuing to work her open.

Once satisfied that she was ready, he slipped his fingers out and picked up the plug. Demetrius grabbed one cheek and pulled, exposing her completely. Then, he pressed the plug to the tight hole, pushing gently until it penetrated her.

He worked the plug in and out, rocking it deeper until it finally slipped inside of her, the entrance snapping shut snugly around the narrow stem. "There, now, was that so bad? Judging from your reaction, I think you liked that, didn't you? If there's a whore inside of you, Bunny, I'm going to drag her out kicking and screaming. I promise you that."

She didn't respond, instead squeezing and releasing, focusing on the weight inside of her, surprised to find that the fullness still made her core tingle with need. Would she break so easily? Bend to his will this quickly? And how could she possibly feel pleasure when she was so full of fury and fear? She had never felt so betrayed by her own body.

Demetrius wiped his hand off on a towel he pulled from the box. She could see its contents if she looked but quickly decided that she didn't want to know what else he had in store. Bunny hated surprises, and she wanted to hate this, too.

Without any warning, Demetrius slapped her ass, and she yelped in response. The impact drove the plug deeper into her. "Sit up, Bunny. Put your back to my chest." His command rang clear in the still air.

She slowly got up, still getting used to the feeling of fullness. Twisting gently, Bunny sat stiffly in his lap, but he tugged her against him so that her back pressed against his firm chest.

Her heart was racing as sweat beaded on her forehead. Bunny could feel his hard cock even through his pants, pressing into her ass. But she could also feel her captor's racing heart through her back. He was enjoying this. Too much, in her opinion.

Bunny gulped, shivering again, but this time from the fearfulness her indignation had been concealing.

His hands rose to her breasts, cupping them gently, pointer and thumb pinching around either nipple. He moved his fingers softly back and forth, working the little peaks until they began firming from his attention.

Bunny's teeth clenched as she began the next battle against reacting to his affections. Her tits had always been hyper-sensitive; she could come simply from an expert pair of hands working them.

If she could say anything positive about the sociopath behind her, it was that his hands were clearly experienced in the art. Despite her best efforts she could feel herself responding immediately. The gentle pulse in her pussy began to flutter, her clit swelling as her wetness betrayed her arousal.

Demetrius put his lips to the nape of her neck before whispering, "That's my girl."

She gasped at the feeling of warm breath blowing gently across her skin, before growling,

"I'm not your fucking girl." He laughed darkly in response, a hand slipping down between her legs.

"That pretty little pussy of yours says differently." She felt his fingers spread her labia, his pointer finger dragging slowly up her slit, before coming to a rest on her clit. "My, my, are you wet for me." Then, using her wetness, Demetrius began circling the small bud, causing Bunny to wriggle as her teeth ground.

She didn't want this. She *didn't*.

A raspy moan escaped her reddened lips, swollen with desire even as her brain railed against the reaction. The soft flutter between her legs had turned into a desperate pounding.

Although she wouldn't describe herself as hypersexual, others absolutely would, and had. It didn't take much to "bring out the whore in her," as Demetrius had put it.

With one hand pinching and rubbing a nipple and the other expertly working her clit, she knew an orgasm was imminent. She was clenching involuntarily around the plug, stimulating herself further. As much as she fought the rising tide threatening to engulf her, it was inevitable that she would be pulled out to sea.

She fought it, but part of her needed it; she was desperate for that tide to roll in and extinguish the searing need burning in her throbbing core. It was only made worse by the fullness in her ass, the plug being jostled by her frantic writhing.

And then, Demetrius stopped entirely.

Bunny gasped, freezing, and his soft chuckle tickled her ear. "What? Do you want me to keep going? Did you enjoy that, you little whore?" The whisper was nearly inaudible.

"Fuck you, you sociopathic piece of shit." She panted back, nipples swollen and pussy still begging for more. Her body was covered in a thin sheen of sweat, hands clenching him mid-thigh. Bunny could feel shame and anger crowding in. She was furious with herself for giving him the satisfaction of a reaction. *I'm only doing this because it's better to cooperate,* she reminded herself, *I only have to pretend to like this until help arrives.*

Against her better judgment, she was still intent on believing that somebody was coming to rescue her. She knew that the first 48 hours after being kidnapped were the most critical. Unfortunately, that window was closing quickly.

He had taken her the previous morning. That meant there was a little less than a day left at best. Bunny hadn't seen any clocks and there were no windows, leaving her disoriented.

Demetrius reached under her arm and moved upward to wrap around the front of her throat. She felt his warm breath tickle her ear, sending sparks up her spine. "Stand up."

Without hesitation, she leaped from his lap, stumbling slightly from the headrush. Her blood had pooled between her legs, leaving her dizzy with unwanted desire.

Demetrius stood, uncomfortably close, and ran a hand across the small of her back as he sidestepped around her. He then moved to the recessed shelving. Bunny watched him wearily while he rooted around one of the drawers, pulling out two long leather straps. They looked like collars, with silver buckles on the ends and large rings down their lengths.

Demetrius turned, inky eyes boring into hers. She felt another flush reddening her face and her eyes dove to the side, desperate to look anywhere but his face.

Without a word, he walked to her and knelt at her feet, and Bunny found a new opportunity to prod him.

"The next time you're on your knees will also be because of me," She snarled, teeth flashing as her face twisted with anger, "Because I'm going to ensure my testimony sends you to prison for the rest of your life." Bunny was taking chances, her anger getting the best of her.

His smile was wicked. "No, Bunny. The

next time I'm on my knees will be because I'm burying my face in that gorgeous pussy while you scream and beg."

She sneered in response.

Demetrius wrapped the straps around her thighs and buckled them securely. He then stood, reaching a hand out to pinch her chin once more between his pointer finger and thumb.

"Little Bunny, you're never getting out of here. You are mine. I own your body, and when I'm finished, I'll have your mind, too. You're going to be addicted to the way I fuck you."

He was full of shit. She would never submit to him. Bunny's mind had always been her own, even when it was the only thing she had. She wouldn't give that up to anybody.

Demetrius looped a finger through the ring at the front of her collar, pulling her toward the bed. *Another sign he's a veritable psycho,* she thought grimly, *Who the hell places a bed like that?* It wasn't touching any of the walls.

Despite her desperation to ignore it and think of anything else, her pussy still strummed with an unbearable yearning for release.

Demetrius opened a drawer on the bedside table and pulled out a vibrator and dildo. He threw them on the bed, a pair of leather wristbands following shortly. Then, he crawled to the center and slid back, leaning slightly against the velvet headboard.

"Come here, Bunny. Lay on your back on top of me." He purred, a smirk growing.

She did as she was told, laying on her back, her legs between his, back pressed once more into his muscular chest. Her heart was pounding steadily, skipping beats now and again. The disconnect between her body and mind left an inner war waging, and Bunny couldn't help but feel her mind was losing.

He pulled her arms up to her chest, wrapping the bands around her wrists and buckling them. They had clips hanging off of them that she noticed with growing concern. Demetrius then pulled her hands to rest on either side of her and clipped her wrists to the straps around her thighs. The black leather stood out starkly against her milky skin.

Her mind gained ground in the war as she realized with horror that she had lost control of a set of extremities. There would be no fighting back with her hands.

Demetrius brought his hands to her breasts, rubbing and massaging her nipples until she began writhing, straining against the explosive pleasure sending shockwaves through her stomach, and into her center.

"That's it, Bunny. Let go. I know you want this, even if you're stubborn."

She gritted her teeth, concentrating on staying still, furious with herself for betraying her body's involuntary reactions to his touch.

Demetrius stopped, reaching over for the vibrator, and lifted his legs so that they lay over the tops of hers. He used his heels to pry her legs apart. She tried to snap them together on instinct only to find that they were firmly pinned in place.

Her kidnapper had muscles of steel even compared to her relatively high lower body strength. She was now truly helpless and bared to him completely. A familiar buzz sounded next to her ear and Bunny sucked in a sharp breath.

A thought bloomed. How often had she dreamed of forced orgasms given mercilessly by a gentle yet ruthless man? She railed against it. At one point, she had wanted that. But not like this.

In the next moment, the vibrator was placed firmly against her clit, and she felt a rise of sensation that sent her reeling. It was on a blessedly low setting that allowed her to resist moving even as he began tapping it up and down, obviously trying to elicit a reaction.

"The first rule is that you are never to come without my permission. Your pleasure is mine to give and take as I please, Bunny. You don't get to decide when you finish anymore," He whispered before pulling her earlobe between his teeth, stopping to say, "But we'll see how long you last. I think you're going to break."

"As though I'd ever give you that satisfaction." She spat, but her confidence was a facade. Bunny had always been sensitive and capable of multiple back-to-back orgasms. When she touched herself, she could reach her climax within seconds. She hadn't ever exercised self-control over her pleasure..

Now, she desperately wished she had tried edging… but it wasn't like she was planning on being kidnapped by a sexual deviant with sinister intentions, and she had never understood why you'd deny yourself the peak of pleasure when it was so accessible. Stamina was never something she concerned herself with.

"We'll see." He laughed mirthlessly before punching the button on the side of the vibrator to a higher setting. She immediately felt the effects as the walls of her pussy began to flutter. Bunny growled, hunching her shoulders and pressing her back into his chest. Her eyes were pinched shut and her teeth were bared. She was concentrating on the strenuous task of denying her body something she had always given freely.

After a few moments, Demetrius hummed

thoughtfully to himself, he pulled the vibrator away and placed it on the bed where it continued to buzz. It was once a delightful sound but now it rang out like a threat.

Next, he placed the tip of the dildo at her entrance, rubbing the tip up and down her slit. She noticed immediately that it was huge. Easily eight inches, with a thick girth that her chest and core tightened at the sight of.

"Get ready, Bunny. Things are about to get… difficult for you, I imagine." Demetrius murmured, before beginning to work the tip in and out of her. He slid it in a little more each time until it sunk into her up to the hilt. She was panting with effort as she strained to accept the toy.

It stretched her in a way that would normally be delightful. Combined with the plug weighing heavily in her ass, she was deliciously full and fighting against her own lust.

He then began thrusting it in and out of her, keeping a steady rhythm as his other hand lifted to a nipple. *Oh, God, no, please,* she thought to herself, eyes widening wildly as the burning need in her pussy grew to a fever pitch.

He stopped, leaving it fully inserted.

The vibrator was suddenly back, pressing firmly against her clit, and his fingers were still toying expertly with her nipple. She was writhing, jerking her legs in an effort to close them to no avail. His powerfully built body kept her spread effortlessly, even in the face of her struggle.

It was infuriating how easy this seemed to him. He didn't even sound like he was exerting himself; his breathing was even and steady despite her frantic wrestling for freedom.

Bunny's pussy was swelling, wetness spreading across the sheets. She was quickly coming undone, so close to breaking his rule.

"How about something new to help move things along?" He asked in a pleasant tone that made her squirm. It was casual, as though suggesting a restaurant they had never tried.

Bunny was relieved of the vibrator, and she let loose a gasp before she could stop herself.

The reprieve was short-lived, however. He leaned over, stretching across the bed to grab something from the drawer. When he leaned back, his hands came around to her front, and she glanced down to notice wicked-looking nipple clamps in his hands.

Her eyes widened, panic rising in her tight throat. In a few seconds, her nipples were being pleasantly pinched in a vicious grip.

"There we go." He murmured, pleased with himself. He rubbed the pad of his pointer finger over the apex of a nipple, grinning as she jerked away from the touch that left her feeling absolutely electric.

Without warning, the vibrator was back, and her mouth was gaping, eyes wide as her hips wriggled under the strain.

"Please, please no," She whimpered, shaking her head from side to side, "Please stop. I can't." Her words were short and choppy as she steeped in disgust at the unwanted desire drowning out her thoughts.

"Remember, Bunny, you are not to come without permission. You need to learn how to control yourself. You can do this, I promise. Just breathe through it."

Even as he said the words directly into her ear, Bunny could hardly hear him. Her head was swimming, the crushing weight of pleasure threatening to destroy her self-control.

He grabbed her midsection to still her, hitching his thighs so that he could pin her hips and keep them still. Without the ability to wriggle away from the harsh buzz of the vibrator, it wouldn't be long until she was sent flying over the edge into oblivion.

Bunny began crying out. It was senseless babbling, begging him to stop, pleading with him that she couldn't follow his stupid fucking rule when he was doing his best to force her into breaking it, setting her up to fail. The worst part was the knowledge that he had planned this, he was fully aware that she would not be able to follow his directions. This bastard man wanted her to earn the punishment he had in mind, through whatever means necessary.

And so it happened. She lost the war.

Chapter Five

Bunny's vision went blurry and her lips parted with an earth-shattering scream. She felt powerful shockwaves exploding through her pussy as it rippled with a powerful orgasm.

Tears of rage flooded her raw eyes as she gasped for breath, desperate for more stimulation and hating herself for it.

Demetrius simply sighed, pulling the vibrator away from her. "Well, if you want to come that badly, let's give you what you want." His voice was even and smooth, but something sinister lurked beneath.

Suddenly, Bunny was rolled over unceremoniously, and left on her stomach as he moved across the bed. She lay there, dildo still stretching her, forehead pressed into the soft bedding as she sobbed softly in frustration.

She heard him get off the bed, and walk

away. When he returned, he knelt over her, knees on either side of her thighs. She felt his hand grip the base of the plug buried in her ass, and he slowly pulled it out.

It was quickly replaced by something much larger. This time he was rougher, sinking it inside of her by rapidly thrusting it back and forth until the ring of muscle snapped around the stem once more. She whimpered at the intrusion. The combination of both massive toys made Bunny feel like she would burst at the seams.

He lifted himself off the bed, wrapping his hand around her waist and lifting her effortlessly into a humiliating carry. She didn't struggle, instead hanging limply, legs closed to keep the dildo in place between her thighs. She didn't want to face his anger if it fell out.

Demetrius was carrying her toward a wide bench fitted with restraints. He bent his knees to drop her onto it, her arms and legs sliding to either side while her torso rested on the wide leather seat.

In the next few moments, she was strapped in tightly by her wrists and ankles with padded cuffs. They stretched her taut toward the ground but not uncomfortably so.

"Since you're apparently so desperate to come, I'll give you what you want. You can come as much as you like now, greedy girl." He sounded far too pleased, and it was the confirmation she needed that he had planned this all along. Bunny swallowed as he bent down with a ball gag in hand. "I don't want to listen to your begging. Open your mouth."

She did without hesitation.

Bunny was still waging war internally, refusing to admit the orgasm signaled defeat. She didn't want this. She *didn't*. But she couldn't stop the physiological reaction her body had.

Demetrius positioned something under the bench. She realized there was a hole right under the top of her pussy. He gently opened her folds and pressed something round to her clit until the pressure was almost painful. She imagined he had secured it in place but wasn't sure through what means, since she couldn't see what he was doing.

What she did know was that this must be a Hitachi wand. She was sure of it.

Her hips shot up to move away from the overwhelming sensation once he turned the toy on, immediately switching to a setting high enough to overwhelm her. Demetrius responded to her attempt at evasion by lifting the last set of straps attached to the bench around her ass, tightening them to hold her hips firmly in place. It moved the plug around as her hips fought for freedom from the stimulation.

There was no escaping the relentless buzzing of the wand. Bunny cried out. A piercing screech ripped from her throat, followed by furious growling.

"You're acting like an animal, Bunny," Demetrius commented, unphased by her frantic cries. "We'll work on your behavior first because you've been incorrigible. Coming without permission, begging, whining, being obstinate... It's almost as though you enjoy being in trouble."

Bunny whipped her head from side to side. The pressure was building in her belly and her nipples throbbed from the clamps that were still pinching them brutally, agitating her as they pressed into the bench.

Demetrius pushed Bunny's chest up so that he could reach a hand under her. In a couple of moments, her nipples were gloriously free.

Unfortunately, the clamps were quickly replaced by the warm swirl of a tongue. Demetrius licked and sucked the tender flesh.

She was being torn in so many directions; her tight ass, her pounding pussy, her burning clit, and now the sucking mouth on her tits.

She couldn't stop herself. She tumbled over the edge again with a scream.

Luckily, Bunny had plenty of experience with climaxing multiple times. She would give them to herself as a stress reliever before bed, usually every night. So even as her pussy pulsed powerfully with orgasm after orgasm, she hung on and rode out each choppy wave.

But, after a few minutes, the assault began to take its toll and Bunny realized that he didn't intend on letting up. Instead, Demetrius leaned down and twisted the dial on the wand, increasing the speed.

Bunny began hyperventilating, eyes wide and pleading as they met his. "It's okay, Bunny. You wanted this, remember?" He whispered, running a finger down her face from temple to chin.

Her eyes rolled to the back of her head as the pleasure slowly morphed into a blinding pain. It was too much. She couldn't do this. She couldn't. Her ass was clamping around the plug which made her feel so full she feared she would split in half. Her pussy was gripping the massive dildo, both desperate for release and cessation of the sensations being forced upon it.

Demetrius suddenly stood up and her heart skipped, hope flooding in. Was it over? When he returned from walking away, her heart quickly fell from the heights of hope to the lowest point in her stomach. He was holding a paddle.

"You didn't think I would let you off easily, did you?" He mused, slapping the paddle onto his hand gently as he studied her wriggling, sweat-soaked body. The leather bench had become slippery from the wetness leaking from her center and the dripping perspiration.

The paddle then landed harshly on her ass, and she yelped from the sharp pain. On one hand, it was a relief to feel something other than the roaring, intense pleasure. On the other, it was yet another direction in which her struggling mind was pulled.

This couldn't go on for much longer. He was relentlessly slamming the paddle down on her ass as the rest of her body was desperate for the end of this ruthless treatment. The plug buried itself with each impact and she was heaving throaty, desperate moans.

After a few more moments, an eternity for Bunny, Demetrius knelt and turned off the wand. She was screaming so consistently her throat had become raw. He slipped the plug out of her ass..

Demetrius undid the straps and Bunny hung listlessly, entirely spent and close to passing out. He knelt, pushing the hair plastered to her forehead back behind her ear. "You were such a good girl," he murmured, "And I'm so impressed by you. You're so beautiful when you're coming for me, you know that? You did so good for me."

She didn't respond. She couldn't respond. He turned her over surprisingly gently, took the dildo out, and pulled her into a bridal hold, Demetrius then carried her across the room and through a doorway.

It led into an expansive bathroom with a massive soaking tub, the type she previously would have drooled over. Bunny only briefly took in her surroundings before her head turned to rest against his chest, breathing in that smoke anc cedar scent. The cologne was oddly comforting, and she longed for anything to help soothe her.

Demetrius laid her down on the tile and she groaned as the cool floor met her feverish body. Bunny could hear him moving around, turning on the faucet, rustling. She was exhausted and lethargic, so much so that she couldn't even muster the energy to be concerned about what he was doing to her next.

After a few moments, Bunny felt herself being lifted again and realized the rustling she'd heard had been him removing his clothing. He stepped over the edge of the tub and knelt in the rising water, before turning so that they were in the same position as earlier; her back to his chest.

"You're stunning when you're like this, so worn out from playtime," He said, stroking her cheek, "Let's get you cleaned up."

Her muscles were still completely slack, and he moved her around easily.

She felt a soft cloth sliding against her skin and the pleasant smell of body wash flooded the room. It smelt like he did. *I guess that's what he uses,* she thought distantly, *Couldn't even be bothered to get me my own scent.* This seemed like an insane complaint in the grand scheme. Floating high above her body, she didn't care.

The water was blessedly warm and soothed the aches she felt stirring across her entire being. There wasn't a place left untouched.

Demetrius kissed her temple as his hand

moved between her legs, dragging the cloth between her outer labia and inner thigh. She mewled softly as the tender area began to throb.

"Hopefully you learned your lesson," Demetrius said gently, "But then again, seeing you like that… Absolutely unbelievable… Incredible, honestly. I hope you didn't learn a thing." It almost seemed like he was talking to himself rather than her.

The water had filled the tub close to overflowing at this point. Demetrius leaned forward and Bunny was bent under the movement. His muscular arm wrapped around her chest with his hand on the front of her throat to keep her from falling into the water. With a quick twist of his wrist, he turned the faucet off and leaned back.

Then, he turned Bunny around in his lap so that her legs folded and she knelt with a knee on either side of his hips. Demetrius slid an arm around her waist and raised a hand to cup her face. "Y'know, I still haven't had you yet tonight, sweet Bunny."

Demetrius leaned forward and captured her swollen lips with his.

Bunny was still floating above the clouds,

only partially aware of her environment. She was fighting the need to sleep. But, in her dreamy haze, she returned the kiss. Their mouths moved in sync, gentle and slow. His hand had slipped from her cheek to the nape of her neck, pulling her closer to deepen their connection.

She sighed into his mouth, and he groaned in response.

Pulling away, he whispered, "Such a good girl for me…" before holding the back of her head with his finger threaded through her hair.

Bunny could feel his hard length pressing into her slit and realized he had likely chosen the dildo to prepare her for his size. His manhood was impressive, judging by the feeling of it against her body.

With a smooth motion, he lifted her hips and held her so that his tip rested at her entrance.

"Do you want this, Bunny? Do you want my cock inside of you?" He asked, sounding strangely genuine. She thought for a moment, trying to formulate an opinion, grabbing for even a single cohesive thought in her spinning head. Her pussy was somehow still begging for more, even as discomfort drummed.

"Yes," She admitted in a whimper, panting

once again from the headrush of the hot water and another wave of desire building in her belly. It shocked her that her body could still betray her, even after he had tortured her so thoroughly.

With that answer, he put his hand between her legs to spread her pussy before slowly lowering her body onto his length until he filled her to the hilt.

Demetrius' head fell back and he gasped. "So tight, my God," he groaned hoarsely, "You feel so good…. Fuck." He began lifting her up and down by her hips, while her arms moved to encircle his neck, tits pressed into his face.

And then, she found a burst of energy she didn't know she had left. If the bastard was going to take her, she was in control this time. Fuck the bastard. He couldn't have her pleasure. Instead, she'd take it from him. Bunny began grinding while rising and lowering.

He tensed, startled by the change of pace, and then his head dropped back and Demetrius moaned. "Slow down, Bunny," He gasped.
She wouldn't.

Instead, Bunny picked up the pace, furiously riding him until he was whimpering. She almost stopped short when the noises began escaping his slightly parted lips but managed to keep the same rhythm.

And then she gritted her teeth, rage flashing in her chest at his wanton display. This wasn't for him. It was for *her*. It was a way to take back control, to exert dominance. His pathetic whimpers meant it was working, but she hated that he was enjoying it.

He didn't understand what she was doing. She wanted him to know, to acknowledge that he didn't own her while she was using him like this.

Bunny leaned her face around the side of his head as he began to quake, close to the finish line, and whispered into his ear, "I want you to know that I'm just using you as a human dildo, you fucking sicko. You've taken enough tonight. This is for me, do you understand?"

His eyes widened but squeezed shut again quickly as his orgasm ripped through his body. Bunny's followed close behind, more pain than pleasure as the soreness between her legs returned with a vengeance.

She yelped and then collapsed onto his chest, her entire body relaxing. Bunny felt dirty, used, and horrified at the events of the evening. But now, after this, she felt more in control.

She was barely conscious for the rest of the bath, only halfway there when he lifted her from the tub, dried her off, and laid her carefully onto her little nest on the floor.

She did shiver in disgust, however, when he kissed her forehead and said, "Sleep well, Bunny. I think you deserve a treat. You did so well tonight. In the morning, head to the kitchen down the hall and get yourself a coffee. Maybe Michael will to take you on a tour tomorrow."

While she barely heard him, she did register the information. Wasn't Michael supposed to give her that tour today? She was glad he hadn't. She couldn't stand the idea of anybody seeing her like this; used, broken, spent.

He left. Bunny fell into a deep, dead sleep.

Chapter Six

Her pussy throbbed with the memory of the previous night, nipples equally tender. There wasn't a part of her that wasn't aching from her captor's torment. She was curled up in her bed, wrapped in the blanket that was increasingly becoming an object of comfort for her. There were so few of those in this place. She would take what she could get.

While it was a relief to know she could at least have the normalcy of coffee, she wished it was from the little cafe she liked to frequent. There, she had made plans to travel abroad before graduate school, dreaming of the misted mountains and far-reaching forests that awaited her in Europe. Now, that was a fading aspiration.

Bunny briefly wondered if there was a point in holding onto the promise of rescue. As the hours passed, she could feel herself becoming listless with the loss of hope.

Why was he doing this? It was clear Demetrius could have anybody he wanted. She imagined a sea of women were likely falling over themselves for his attention. He was clearly wealthy and though she was loathe to admit it, astonishingly attractive.

But musing over his lack of a consensual love life wasn't how she intended to spend her day. She wanted to thoroughly investigate her spacious surroundings and familiarize herself with any routes of escape she could find.

Standing on shaking legs, Bunny winced as the cool air puckered her nipples. The rule she hated most of all was his insistence on her nudity. It left her feeling unbearably exposed.

Bunny knew it was an effort to break her further. It was obvious that his ultimate goal was turning her into an ideal fuck toy for him to use and abuse as he saw fit.

The worst part was how in line with her fantasies this was. Bunny had plenty of time to think this morning when she woke up. She had realized with a dawning horror that this was exactly what she used to think about when she masturbated. Her fingers would circle her swollen clit as she imagined complete domination.

She'd come hard to the idea of a collar and a simple life free of responsibility, unrestrained for once in her sexuality as she explored the burgeoning depths of darkness in her fantasies. Her therapist had told her this was normal for trauma survivors, that it was often the brain's effort to take back control that had been snatched away. It had taken her years to work up the courage to bring up sex during their sessions.

Bunny had always felt dirty concerning sensuality of any sort, the assaults she had faced in her childhood left scars deeply dug into her psyche. It was originally her intention to reopen these wounds, to bleed for the sake of healing. But, after a few trauma sessions, her therapist suggested they let sleeping dogs lie.

Sometimes trauma didn't have a resolution, and that was okay. It could be more damaging to attempt revisiting the horrors that haunted you than to simply try and leave things as they were and move forward.
That was fine by her. It hurt so fiercely when she though about it, she thought she'd die.

Bunny snapped out of her reverie. This wasn't the time for psychoanalyzing herself or reminiscing about sessions spent with soaked tissues on a soft couch.

She needed coffee and a plan.

The door opened into a long hallway. Bunny poked her head out to ensure it was empty and slipped out of her room undetected. The goal was to remain invisible to her captors.

She shuddered to think of either one seeing her in such a vulnerable state, even if Demetrius had already known her so carnally and Michael had witnessed her nudity the previous day. Besides, if they saw her they might question her incessant ferreting as she attempted to find ways to break free of this prison.

Her bare feet padded gently along the plush carpet, a welcome change from the wood in the bedroom. It was mercifully soft on her sore soles. The chase through the forest had left her in pain. Winter still had a hold on the ground, making it hard and unrelenting during the hunt.

The cavernous kitchen seemed to be empty of either assailant. With the coast clear, Bunny breathed a little sigh of relief and rushed to the black marble counters. There were mugs on a rack. Her hands were still shaking as she plucked one off and placed it under the spout of the automatic coffee maker before popping in a pod and pressing the brew button.

Bunny's head had begun aching again and this time she suspected it was from caffeine withdrawal. Like most adults, she was an avid consumer of the beverage, it had become a comforting start to her busy days.

She opened the fridge to locate milk or creamer, and almost dropped a glass bottle she had pulled out when she heard a voice. "Finding everything okay?"

She whipped around to see Demetrius, arms crossed, leaning casually in the doorway. She tensed. "Yes, thank you." A quiet response she hoped would satisfy him.

"Make me a cup when you're finished. Two teaspoons of sugar, and two tablespoons of creamer. You'll bring it to me in my study, at the other end of the hall."

He turned and walked down the hallway in the opposite direction from the bedroom without another word, leaving Bunny speechless and bristling.

Was it not enough to violate her? Did he have to make her his servant, as well? Her face was flushed and her hands shook. This situation had stoked her ire in a way nothing else had as far as she could remember.

Besides, who the hell measured their creamer and sugar so exactly? *Fucking sociopath behavior,* She thought to herself.

Bunny realized her coffee cup was full and the machine had stopped dispensing. She pulled the mug from under the spout, deciding on a black cup rather than using the creamer she had found. The bitterness of the brew suited her mood. She then set about making another.

Once she was done, Bunny walked confidently down the hall and into his study. If he wanted coffee, the bastard could have it. He looked up at her with an infuriating smirk.

Bunny walked over and promptly poured the cup out into his lap.

Demetrius roared in pain as the steaming liquid seeped into his black slacks. She immediately regretted the rashness of her decision, even as she felt satisfaction at causing Demetrius even a fraction of the pain he had inflicted on her.

In an instant, she was on the floor, his hand gripped around her neck, his face millimeters from hers. His onyx eyes were lit up with a terrifying intensity she had not yet seen from him.

"You fucking bitch." He hissed, constricting her breathing and leaning up. His other hand whipped back, and then landed hard across her cheek.

Even with his iron grip restricting her movement, Bunny felt her head jerk from the impact.

Searing pain exploded through her face and a strangled howl erupted from her mouth. Her hands were around his wrist, nails digging deep in his flesh. She wasn't entirely sure why she was trying to dislodge him. With any luck, maybe he'd decide just to kill her. Bunny was no stranger to suicidality and was sure death would be a welcome exit from this horror show.

With a grunt, Demetrius stood, never loosening his grip as he brought her with him.

He dragged her over to the chaise lounge next to towering bookcases built into the wall. Bunny briefly admired them. The range of colored spines surprised her. She would have imagined he'd want a more cohesive aesthetic.

And then the realization that she was dissociating slammed her back into reality.

Demetrius sat down heavily and yanked her over his lap. She knew immediately where this was going, and fear began to pool in her stomach. He hadn't been gentle previously, but this was different. Right now he was enraged. Surely that would factor into how hard he was about to beat her.

She braced herself, breath ragged as she whimpered with anticipation. As expected, his hand landed heavy on her ass. It was sheer agony, blow after blow sending sharp pain rippling through her ass.

But it didn't last nearly as long as she thought. After a few blows, and once she was sobbing into the velvet cushion, she felt a coolness on her backside. She felt his fingers working whatever it was into her skin.

"W-what are you doing?" She sobbed, hiccuping through the sentence. A burning shame filled her body. Not only was she entirely exposed and humiliated, but now she felt horribly weak at her captor's mercy.

"It's a lotion infused with lidocaine. It'll

make you less sore," He snapped.

Bunny felt immediate confusion. Lidocaine was a numbing agent. She had assumed part of the punishment would be the soreness she felt after the spanking. However, the lotion kicked in almost immediately and there was a little relief from the stinging.

Then, Demetrius threaded his fingers deep into her mussed hair with his clean hand, yanking her head back so that her back was painfully arched.

His lips to her ear, Demetrius whispered, "Don't ever do that shit again, or I'll tie you up spread eagle and let all of my friends have free reign with you to do whatever they want."

Bunny sucked in a fearful breath.

"Do you understand?" He barked, jerking her head back. She wailed before frantically struggling to shake her head in confirmation.

"Good girl. Go drink your coffee and get something to eat. I still have a surprise for you today." With that, he patted her ass, and she felt fury rising in her chest again.

"Demetrius told me about your little…. Accident earlier." Again, a voice startled her as she attempted to enjoy her coffee in silence.

Michael.

She blushed deeply, crossing her arms over her breasts and crossing her legs in what she hoped was a casual gesture instead of a desperate measure. "What do you want?" She asked flatly, staring daggers at the person she had formerly thought of as her shot at rescue.

"Wow, hey, don't get mad at me," He said with a laugh, "I'm not the one who decided it would be a good idea to fuck with Demetrius. I have to hand it to you, though. You've got balls of absolute steel, girl."

Bunny stared at him incredulously. She didn't find anything about this funny. "It wasn't an accident," She growled, "I did it on purpose."

"Well, yeah. Obviously. But I'm still going to call it an accident because the alternative is that you're dumb as hell… And I doubt that's the case." He said briskly, before pausing his speech as he walked toward the coffee machine.

She narrowed her eyes, tracking him as he strode across the room. As he began pulling together his coffee, he broke the silence again.

"Hell hath no fury like a woman scorned, right?"

"Are you seriously trying to make conversation with me?" She snapped.

He sighed heavily. "Look, I know this is… a lot. I get it. I'm not happy about it, either. Demetrius is a real fucking fucker. I know that better than anybody," He paused and glanced at her before continuing, "Well, except you."

"Then why do you work for him?" Her exasperation was clear.

"Well, uh, this is going to make me sound like a real piece of shit. And, honestly, I kind of am," He sighed, "The truth is, I like money. A lot. And Demetrius provides that. I'm not much of a good person, but at least I can admit it."

Bunny just stared at him, mouth gaping. "Are you serious? How morally bankrupt do you have to be before you're willing to let somebody do this for some quick cash?" She waved her hands at her naked body.

"I've filed at least three times in my life, as it turns out!" He quipped, winking.
Bunny screamed, turning and storming out.

"Hey, wait! What about the tour?" He called after her, and when she didn't bother to respond he followed it with "At least be ready for the surprise, Barbara! You're going to love it!"

She didn't give a shit about the "surprise." And she was certain she would, in fact, not like it. And she was suddenly fine with him calling her by her full name. The man was just as much of a psycho as Demetrius, and he could get fucked.

Chapter Seven

As stereotypical as it was, Bunny had always felt at home in a barn. Little girls were known for their equine obsessions; most women could recall having at least a phase where they begged their parents for a pony before it petered out as they grew.

For Bunny, that phase grew into a passion. The liberty she felt while astride a horse thrilled her in a way that was all too addictive. There was something magical about the animals. Their ability to understand human emotion and respond to their riders was incredible. She had been working with and riding horses since she was a young child, growing up as a barn rat that her trainers couldn't get rid of. It taught her discipline, responsibility, and dedication.

These were lessons Bunny took with her through life and had helped her achieve the things she didn't think were possible.

Besides her freedom, she missed her horse. Her entire life she had dreamed of the day she could own instead of leasing lesson horses. It was another goal she considered a pipe dream. However, the year before she had buckled down and saved money until she could afford to import a Danish Warmblood. He was her pride and joy.

Contrary to popular belief, importing was often cheaper to obtain higher-quality horses. The abundance of prestigious lines and native breeds in Europe provided a better selection for young equestrians looking to move up the levels. Bunny was one such equestrian.

So, when Demetrius came to her with breeches, tall boots, and a polo, she felt an overwhelming rush of emotion. First of all, she no longer had to be naked. Second of all, what game was he playing now? And how did he know about her affinity for horses?

She imagined he had been watching her for some time before taking her, it wouldn't make sense for this specific man to kidnap a random woman. No, he was more careful than that, more selective. She couldn't imagine he did much of anything without a plan of action and copious research to back himself up.

Regardless, she was going to ride, and nobody could take that joy from her.

"You're really gonna love this, Bar-Bunny, sorry," Michael threw up his hands at the venomous glance she gave him. "Y'know, you sure do have a lot of demands for somebody in no position to be making them." He grumbled, shoving his hands in his pockets while his shoulders tilted and hunched against the brisk morning air.

Bunny wasn't sure as to the exact time, but she could tell it was early morning. Frost still tipped the tall, wild grass framing the walkway the pair strode down. There was a shimmering sheen of mist still clinging to everything in sight.

It happened to be her favorite time of day.

She had countless fond memories of waking up while the sun was still asleep, getting ready for the day, and then driving to the barn while the sky faded from charcoal to dusty purple and soft pink. It was a peaceful time when she kept company only with her thoughts and the beautiful animals she worked with. She was the only one there to break the silence.

But the silence was the reason she loved it, so she left it in tact. Bunny reveled in the peace it provided. So, frankly, she wished Michael would shut the fuck up and stop filling the tense space between them with words.

"We're taking his favorite car today. Apparently, Demetrius wants you to have the best of the best, isn't that nice? Thoughtful of the guy. He certainly doesn't think of me and what I want, so you should feel special-" His voice stopped short as her movement did.

Bunny turned her head to look him in the eyes and said, "Michael? Do me a favor and shut the fuck up, okay?" Before starting forward again.

"Jesus… alright.." The man grumbled. Even so, he acquiesced to her demand.

They turned a corner in the path and a few feet ahead was a small parking lot, Demetrius standing beside a sleek, black car.

Her cheeks burned, the flush burning and uncomfortable. All she could think about was the way he had pulled her effortlessly over his knee… how he had used and abused her just the night before. Desire raged against embarrassment in her mind while she became unbearably hot.

Demetrius was wearing a riding habit of his own; tall boots, well-fitted breeches, and a shirt that clung to his musculature. He looked like a brooding model. But she wasn't attracted to him. She could not be attracted to him. Not when he held her like this.

"Hello, my Bunny." Demetrius purred, a predatory smile complimenting the hungry flash that swept across his face, She noticed then that he was holding a ball gag.

Oh fuck off, Bunny thought, heart beginning to race. She had considered briefly that this could be a chance to escape. Her chances of using this opportunity were dwindling.

"Come." He commanded, pointing to the ground at his feet. Bunny began walking before his voice boomed through the space between them again. "Crawl."

Another spark of fury threatened to light an inferno in her chest. He couldn't be serious.

But he was.

She sank to her knees, wincing as the pebbles once beneath her feet now bit into the skin of her knees through the thin pants. Her palms smarted on the rough surface. Red-faced,

Bunny crawled the distance between them, the sparks of pain in her knees and hands worsening the longer she dragged on. And, of course, she would drag it out as long as possible. Why would she rush to be in the presence of the vile, little worm of a man?

Bunny took a shaky breath and turned her eyes to the ground. A nervousness had begun to bubble in her stomach. He used his thumb to drag her bottom lip down slowly before murmuring, "Open."

When she looked up, she noticed the ball gag in his hands. Thinking better of using the moment to be nasty, Bunny held in her words but opened her mouth. Her jaw trembled with a mix of fear and anger. The ball gag was slipped gently into her mouth and secured. Demetrius then stood up and walked to the trunk, opening it, and gesturing for her to get in.

Bunny's eyes widened to saucers, and then shut to slits. She made a muffled noise of disbelief. She wasn't sure of a lot, but she was sure of one thing: she wasn't going *anywhere* near a fucking trunk.

Demetrius sighed, giving her a weary look. "I don't want to fight you today, Bunny. Just do as you're told. I'll count to ten and you'd better be in that trunk before I'm done." As he counted, he began undoing his belt.

An animalistic sound ripped from her throat, and Bunny decided now was her chance to break free. She moved forward as though she were complying, but then whipped in the other direction and took off full tilt. Bunny ripped the ball gag She heard a yelp and an exclamation, and she hoped it had hit Demetrius.

Hearty laughter then sounded behind her, fading as she put distance between herself and the psycho holding her captive. In the next moment, she could hear the steady beat of his running feet as he gave chase.

The road made things easier, but the clothing she wore did not. Riding boots were not made for running and this pair wasn't well broken in, the leather unyielding around her ankles. She wobbled horribly as she attempted to pick up speed.

Unfortunately for her, Demetrius had a pair that was obviously well broken in and much more suited for the chase. Her heart sank as she heard him closing the distance between them. She spared a look over her shoulder and her eyes widened at how close he had managed to get in that time.

So, she let him get a little closer before stopping short and throwing her shoulder into his chest. The impact threw her on her ass since his large form was still flying forward at full speed.

Apparently, it hurt him too, since Demetrius let loose a sharp cry as he bounced backward, landing on his ass, as well. They stared at each other for a few seconds, and then his eyes narrowed and she gulped.

Well, time to get the fuck out of here,
She thought to herself, turning to take off. Unfortunately, Demetrius quickly recovered and flew at her with rage rivaling the coffee incident.

Within seconds, she was flat on her stomach with his heaving chest pressing firmly into her back. She slapped a hand on the loose gravel road, struggling to gain purchase but only succeeding in rasping her already painful palms against the sharp gravel as he grabbed her arms and dragged them behind her back.

"I'm sorry, I'm so sorry," Her voice was high-pitched, a panicked shrill as she realized her escape attempt had failed. What frightened her wasn't his barrel chest crushing her or how every muscle in his body seemed tense.

What frightened her was that outside of his heavy breathing, Demetrius was silent.

Bunny froze in place, eyes burning as they filled with frustrated tears. She had always been quick on her feet and had the collegiate medals to prove it. Half of her scholarships were from her high school career in track and field. It wasn't even him that beat her; her footwear had bested her this time. She was certain she would be faster than him if conditions were more favorable.

Unfortunately, there was nothing favorable about her current circumstances.

Demetrius finally broke his silence.

"Keep. Your hands. Behind. Your back." It was a deathly whisper laced with venom that dissolved any resolve she had left to escape. She didn't dare to disobey him for fear of his reaction.

Once satisfied that she would comply, Demetrius propped himself on one elbow. Bunny began taking desperate breaths as the pressure on her body lessened. She hadn't realized just how dizzy she was from the lack of oxygen.

A hand wrapped tight around her mouth, and her eyes went wide. It was the same hand connected to the elbow Demetrius supported himself on. With the other, she could feel his belt buckle dig into her back as he undid his pants.

Her desperate breaths turned panicked and something between a shriek and a whimper escaped the almost airtight hold he had on her..

Demetrius pulled his belt loose and promptly sat up so that he was kneeling over her with a knee on either side of her torso. Without another word, the belt was looped around her neck, and he was pulling.

Bunny's hands instinctively flew to her neck. With clawing fingers, she attempted to loosen the tight hold on her windpipe.

She barely noticed him pulling her pants down as she attempted to keep the black spots in her vision at bay. Strings of spit escaped her gaping mouth while her eyes bulged. He was suffocating her.

"You did this to yourself, Bunny. Calm down," Demetrius said over her choking.

From there, he pulled down the zippers on her boots and yanked both off her feet, followed by her breeches. Even while removing her clothing from their current position was awkward, he managed it.

Demetrius swung his leg back over to her other side. Finally, there was blessed relief as he allowed the belt to slacken slightly. Bunny planted her bright red face on the ground, head spinning.

"That's my perfect girl," Demetrius had put his lips next to her head, and she could feel them brushing against the shell of her ear as he spoke, "You're so pretty when you're struggling to breathe, you know that? Maybe next time I'll let you choke on my cock instead of my belt."

Bunny stiffened as she realized he was planning on burying himself inside of her long before her body was ready. She wasn't exactly dripping with desire.

But apparently, Demetrius had planned for this. He stood and pulled her with him using the belt. "Stand still, Bunny," he said before kneeling, putting his hand between her legs to grab the belt that dangled down her back again and pull her head back with it. Then, he placed his mouth at her core.

She yelped at the juxtaposition of his hot breath mixing with the cool morning air. She yelped again as he thrusted his tongue into her slit, running it slowly up to her clit which he began sucking on gently. Bunny lost balance, hands threading into his hair to help hold herself up.

Between his tongue exploring her most sensitive parts and the belt pulling her backward, she was more than unsteady. The hold she had on him only served to grind her sensitive cunt into his face, however.

Warmth collected in her belly as pain, fear, adrenaline, and pleasure mingled. Becoming dizzier and dizzier, Bunny hoped giving into her carnality was ultimately his desired outcome. With a last burst of energy, she began rocking her hips into his face, choked moans gargling up.

Sweet release came in that instant as Demetrius allowed the belt to loosen. It wasn't much slack, but enough so she could think straight again.

Bunny whimpered as her legs began to shake, and Demetrius rewarded her by bringing in his other hand to assist his tongue. She could feel her slick pussy easily accept two of his fingers, which curled deliciously inside of her.

Sensing her instability, Demetrius let go of the belt and wrapped his now free hand around her waist to help keep her standing. He then continued to work her, swirling his tongue around her sensitive bud while keeping his fingers busy twisting and curling and thrusting.

She practically howled with frustrated pleasure, furious that her body was once more betraying her arousal. This was all wrong. It was so wrong. Demetrius paused his ministrations for a moment to speak.

"See? I told you next time I was on my knees it would be to make you scream for me," Even as his belt released its tyrant hold on her neck, Demetrius' charcoal-dark whisper wrapped around her throat like a noose.

He then grabbed her waist and took her to the ground none too gently. In an instant, he was on top of her, his legs parting hers.

"Now you should be ready to take it, naughty girl," Demetrius growled, before sliding himself into her up to the hilt.

She moaned and bucked into his hips, matching his rhythm so he slammed deep inside of her with every thrust. As the heat built in her belly and her pussy began to ache with need, she cried out, "Can- can I come? Please, I need to come, Demetrius"

She felt him pause before he started pounding into her harder than before. "Say it again. Fucking say my name again," He roared. "Demetrius," She wailed into the frosted air, and he granted her permission. As soon as he did, Bunny was in free fall, her entire body wracking as her climax slammed through her.

When he finished, Demetrius gently dressed her, wiped away her tears, and held Bunny tightly in his arms.

"This could be so good for you if you just learned how to let go," He whispered into her soft hair, leaving behind a gentle kiss. She shook and whimpered in response, but clung to him all the same.

When they stood, he helped her, holding Bunny close to his chest while she found her strength again. Even while she accepted his help, Bunny felt the stirrings of shame deep inside her. Or was it pleasure? She was beginning to have a hard time telling the two apart.

The pair walked back to the car side-by-side. Bunny felt spent and leaned on Demetrius to keep from falling back over. Her weary eyes quickly found Michael as they turned the corner into the parking lot.

He was casually looking at absolutely nothing, hands in his pockets, slightly flushed. *Coward. He's an absolute fucking coward,* She thought.

Once they were at the trunk, Demetrius picked her up to place her inside, pausing to cradle her to his chest. Finally, he fastened the ball gag around her head once more.

The trunk slammed and all was dark.

The facility was breathtaking. Bunny stared in awe at the gorgeous arches that marked the entrance to the main barn, clearly crafted with expert care on a limitless budget. If it weren't for the gag, her mouth would have dropped.

Michael stayed behind with the car. Her nose had wrinkled as he lit a cigarette and inhaled deeply, filling the space around them with an acrid scent as he blew the smoke out. Bunny had never been a fan of the smell. It reminded her too much of her childhood home.

She was slightly sore from being jostled in the trunk after the chase down the road, but that was all quickly forgotten as they began walking down the aisle. Each stall had a magnificent animal standing inside of it, all warmbloods. This was the facility of her dreams... But she suspected her captor was about to turn ir into a nightmare.

As though on cue, Demetrius opened a door and grinned viciously at her. "Come along, Bunny." He purred, eyes glinting.

Chapter Eight

The tack room was as stunning as the rest of the facility. Expensive saddles were neatly lined on one wall, the opposing side made up of gleaming wooden lockers. The marble and steel kitchenette to the right was gorgeous. There was no doubt they'd also have a lounge… or two, or three. She'd love to see those rooms.

Bunny snapped out of her starstruck daze when Demetrius cleared his throat, standing in front of a door at the far end of the room. He lifted his hand and used his pointer finger to beckon her forward.

Bunny obliged immediately, even as her stomach began turning. For once, he didn't make her crawl. For this, she was thankful.

They walked into the bathroom and she immediately felt her heart drop deep in her belly. It was a large room with a washer and dryer. But her attention was on the blanket spread on the floor. And then to the toys laid on it.

Did he bring her here just to lift her so he could watch her crash back down into despair?

"Don't look so glum, little Bun'. You're absolutely going to ride today, and probably higher quality horseflesh than you've ever sat on." His voice was quiet but still deafening in the space between them.

When he reached out for her, she flinched, breathing hard through her nose. While she was sure he noticed, Demetrius didn't react to it. Instead, he undid the gag and pulled it.

Bunny worked her jaw a bit, raising a hand to rub the sore joints. She didn't dare speak a word for fear that he'd wrestle her to the ground and put the gag back in place.

Everything was silent for a moment, Bunny looking at him out of the corner of her eye, and Demetrius staring back passively. And then his soft murmur shattered the quiet, "Kneel on the blanket."

Bunny froze for a few seconds. Then, she stiffly shuffled over to the blanket and bent down to get into position. She could feel a subtle flutter between her legs, an aching she quelled by squeezing her thighs together. The tug-of-war between body and mind had began anew.

Demetrius slowly crouched to the floor. His hands were clasped, wrists resting on his knees. "I want to watch you play with yourself, Bunny. You're going to bring yourself to the brink of orgasm three times, and then you're going to take the plug and fill your ass." Bunny's stomach tightened, a horrifying realization dawning as she realized his intentions.

This man planned on making her ride a horse while stuffed with that toy. He was more than a psycho. He was clearly a sadist.

"Do you understand?" He whispered, black eyes boring into her blue-green gaze.

"Yes." She whispered back, unable to break the optical connection between them.

From there, without taking her eyes off his face, she reached over and felt for the vibrator. It was a small thing she knew would likely pack more power than seemed possible.

She took a deep breath before scooting back until her mid-back rested against the wall. Sliding down and bending her knees, she spread her feet so that he had a full view of her still-clothed body. She'd consider it a victory if she could get away with not taking anything off.

God knew not much else was.

Demetrius said nothing, although the corners of his mouth lifted so slightly that she would have missed it if she wasn't scouring his face for approval.

With shaking fingers, Bunny undid the button of her breeches and slid the zipper down slowly. They were smooth as butter and clung beautifully to her skin… which meant she would have to pull them down further than she would have liked to get access to her clit.

Her fingers found the space between skin and pants, pulling until her naked mound appeared, and then even more until her pussy was bared to Demetrius' hungry gaze. The vibrator shook. Not because she had turned it on, but because her hands had begun trembling.

In any other situation, this would have been exceedingly hot. She would be melting under the sultry glare of this brooding suitor.

"You have very little self-control, Bunny. We're going to fix that. If you're a good girl, I might even bring you back here on occasion."

At that, she punched the vibrator's button, a thumb holding it down until it buzzed to life.

"Higher." He whispered, a grin unfurling.

She obeyed, pressing twice more until her pussy began to throb in anticipation, her body betraying her stifled desires.

"Pleasure yourself." Another smokey whisper.

Bunny's head fell back, mouth opening and eyes squeezing shut, as she pressed the tip of the vibrator to her clit. The vibrations were strong enough to be felt in her lower abdomen, which was tightening in anticipation of her growing orgasm.

The burn built, and built, and built.

Without warning, she felt a hand around her wrist, eyes snapping open as she gasped.

Demetrius' face was inches from hers. For a few heartbeats, they were caught in that position, both silent and sizing the other up.

"You almost came, didn't you?" He paused, contemplative while her eyes burned bright with frustration and ire, "I won't stop you from coming again. Next time, there will be consequences."

Her head was swimming with heady desire. Even as the humiliation of being watched washed over her, that shame couldn't overcome the warmth of pleasure pulsating between her shivering legs.

If she was being forced into this, why couldn't she also enjoy it? Why shouldn't she?

Bunny swallowed hard as sweat collected in beads on her forehead. The buzz of the vibrator was now a threatening sound and she dreaded the firm press of it against her swollen clit. Against her better judgment, she slipped it between her legs and was immediately transported to a place of bliss and longing.

Her body began writhing as the pressure built low in her stomach. It made her gasp and whimper as wetness collected between her thighs.

Once the she felt the fire roaring to a blaze in her belly, she stopped stopped, leaving a fierce ache where she longed to be touched.

Bunny lay there, gasping and choking on her own moans as the building pressure inside of her dulled to an urgent throb. She barely registered Demetrius sliding behind her so that she was leaning against his chest. He gently tucked a strand of ginger hair behind her ear, leaning forward to whisper.

"That's my good girl. See? I knew you could do it." His warm breath tickled her ear and need flared. She whimpered when he took an earlobe into his mouth, gently nibbling as his hands reached around to rub her nipples through her polo and sports bra.

"Please…" Her voice was hoarse and she cleared her throat immediately after.

What am I doing? This is so wrong. Bunny whined internally, the war inside her coming to a head. This man had kidnapped her, brutalized her, humiliated her, and committed countless unspeakable acts.

Why was she melting under his touch? "Keep going, Bunny. Twice more." He murmured, sliding her shirt up so that it rested on top of her tits. Demetrius popped them out of her bra and began pinching them as Bunny mewled under his ministrations. It was intoxicating. It was delicious. It was fucked up. But so was she.

Her hand dragged down to her center, and she pleasured herself with shaking, sweaty hands as Demetrius continued to murmur words of praise and encouragement in her ear.

Once she had done as he had bidden her, her hand dropped to the ground. Her entire body was shaking with hunger. She wanted more, *needed* more. He was obviously intent, however, on leaving her wanting for release.

She let her head drop back against his shoulder, leaning so her lips were at his neck. That heady scent that was entirely his made her head spin. Was this Stockholm syndrome? She couldn't help but think he was forcing her fragile mind into associating him with pleasure.

If he was, it was working.

Bunny pressed her lips gently to his pulse point before whispering, "Please, please more, Demetrius. I need it." Immediately, he froze. He then relaxed and turned his head to kiss her forehead. "No, you don't, Bunny. You don't need it. You want it."

She groaned in response.

"Time to move on. Get on your back with your legs spread so I can see that pretty, little ass. I want you to put that plug inside of you, and I want to watch." Demetrius began pinching and teasing her nipples again as he detailed his orders.

Face flushing, Bunny slowly pushed herself up onto her knees and removed her breeches entirely. She reached over for the toy and lube and then twisted onto her back so her body was resting between his legs, feet planted on either side of his thighs. If he wanted a show, he could fucking have one. Perhaps if she played along, she could earn his trust.

With trust would come opportunity.

Coating her long fingers, Bunny stared him in the eye even as her face burned and her chest tightened with embarrassment. Then, they slipped between her legs and past her center.

She made quick work of herself, slipping one finger inside, and then a second, scissoring and twisting them as best she could in the awkward position.

While it would have been easier to ready herself more, she relished in the pinching and discomfort that came with sliding a toy inside of her ass while she was still a little tight. The pain underlined the pleasure.

Bunny winced as she pushed it past the ring of muscle that fought to keep it outside. Rocking it back and forth, Bunny bit her lip gently and let her eyes flutter as a throaty moan bubbled up through her chest.

His muscular hands massaged her calves and his breathing had become decidedly heavier. Finally, the plug slid in and her muscles snapped around the stem.

"Look at how good you did," He purred, a smile barely lifting the corners of his lips, "Now, let's go get your reward."

Bunny was suddenly terrified at the prospect of riding for the first time in her life.

Chapter Nine

Bunny followed Demetrius out of the tack room into the regal aisle housing animals she had previously only dreamed of sitting on.

The only sounds were horses softly munching on hay and the occasional swishing tail. It was pure bliss after she had been living a seemingly neverending nightmare. The sweet scent of grain and second-cut hay was rich in the air, mingling with leather and horse sweat.

"Pick one." Demetrius broke the quiet, stopping with his hands clasped behind his back.

"Excuse me?" She said, coming to a sudden halt to avoid running into him. The plug sat heavy inside of her and she was still warm with desperate need between her legs.

"You get to pick any one of them you like. Take your time and feel free to go in the stall with them. There's no rush. This is your treat."

His voice was as soft as ever. He was not the type of man who needed to raise it. She suspected he was used to prompt obedience from others without having to resort to yelling.

Her heart was beating harder. This was everything she had ever wanted, handed to her on a platter. After a moment, though, her heart was sinking in her chest. Demetrius turned his head around to look at her from the corner of his eye. "Are you not pleased?" His voice was tight, riding on the line of annoyance.

"No, no I just- It's a complicated situation," She whispered, throat tightening as reality crashed around her.

"Hm." The only response.

Before he had a chance to change his mind, Bunny turned on heel and walked as quickly as was appropriate for a barn to the stall at the head of the aisle. The horse had caught her eye. She had a soft spot for a beautiful grey, especially one frosted with deep, dark dapples.

Bunny clucked her tongue to get his attention and the magnificent animal lifted his head, jaw working the hay he had pulled into his mouth. It was best to ensure a horse's attention was on you before entering a stall; you don't want to be stuck in a small room with a startled horse.

Once his eyes were safely on her, she opened the stall door and stepped onto the cedar shavings on the stall floor. The scent was divine. His bedding was so thick that her boots sunk in.

The nameplate said, "Maximus."

"Hi, baby," Bunny crooned, holding the back of her hand to his nose. Maximus breathed in her scent as his kind eyes studied her face. He had a gorgeous Roman nose and a thick neck. She loved how he was put together- a perfect example of desired confirmation.

She immediately decided that this was the one she wanted to ride today.

Bunny leaned out of the stall door and snatched the leather halter and lead rope When she went to slide it over his head, the stallion flung it upwards.

"Absolutely not, fucker," She growled, jumping up and curving her hand over the middle of his nose. Holding firmly until she could feel the bone, she pulled him back down and got the halter secured. It was annoying, and she could tell this horse would be fresh. Bunny didn't mind. She liked a challenge.

To be safe, she slid the shank chain

through the halter, over his nose, and out the other side. Once it was clipped in place, she gave them enough slack for him to have his head and walked out of the stall.

Maximus pranced next to her but she paid him no mind. It was all for show. You couldn't punish a stallion for doing what it was born to do. This was a high-energy athlete who loved his job, and he knew it was time to go to work.

She led him to the cross-ties, throwing the lead rope over his neck just in case.

"I assume all of his supplies are in his trunk?" Bunny called cooly down the aisle to Demetrius, who was in a stall grabbing his own mount.

"They are, yes." Came the short reply.

With that, she moved over to the elegant, wooden tack box. It was tall enough to come up to her waist and as ornate as she had ever seen. The cherry wood was seamless, a gold nameplate proudly displaying the horse's show name: Maximum Overdrive.

As she flung open the locking mechanism, Bunny let out a yelp and jerked her hips forward. An incredible buzzing had come to life in her ass. A dark chuckle echoed through the cavernous aisle and her head whipped around, lips pursed and eyes alight with anger.

"I suppose I forgot to mention that," Demetrius said, flashing a dazzling smile. Bunny breathed hard through her nose, shaking slightly once more as hunger flared in her belly and desire began welling. In her excitement, she had somehow forgotten about the toy filling her.

Tacking up went smoothly without any interruptions of the vibratory type. First, she briskly whisked away dust using a dandy brush. She wasn't sure this animal had ever needed a curry in his life, which was incredible considering he was older and lighter because of it.

Dappled gray horses "greyed out" as they aged. This meant that they lost their dappling the older they became. She would guess he was around six, but she hadn't checked his teeth. She could always just ask Demetrius… but she'd rather stick nine-inch nails in her eyes than willingly speak to the psycho.

Once she had picked his hooves and checked his legs over, she saw Demetrius approaching from the corner of her eye. He had a handsome brown saddle draped over his forearm with the matching bridle hanging on his shoulder. The tack was gorgeous.

"Be careful when you cinch his girth. He likes to bite." His tone was casual, and it made her weary. She didn't like the idea of relaxing her guard around him. Although she had originally attempted to humanize herself in his eyes, Bunny had begun to suspect that she was already fully human to Demetrius.

It made the entire situation even stranger. If he didn't see her as a possession, a prize, then how could he stomach the torment he was putting her through?

Snapping out of her thoughts, Bunny turned to the horse as Demetrius arranged the tack on the saddle rack attached to his stall. He walked away without another another word.

Bunny plucked the saddle pad up, placing it so that it was high on his withers. She plopped the saddle on top and slid both back, smoothing the hair on his back, before pulling the front of the pad to tent it so it wouldn't pinch his withers.

Maximus swung his head around and pinned his ears as Demetrius had warned when she began doing up the girth. "Don't even fucking think about it," Bunny grumbled, turning to stare him down threateningly.

The horse seemed to think better of it and contented himself with pinned ears and snapping teeth instead. Bunny wasn't one to make a fuss where it was unnecessary. So long as he wasn't truly intending to bite her, she wouldn't react.

Once ready, she slipped the reins over Maximus' head and followed Demetrius outside. Michael lounged like a lazy cat on a chair in front of the arena, taking long drags of a cigarette.

She briefly wondered how many that made today. Maybe if she was lucky his lungs would shrivel up and she could make her escape while Demetrius tried to revive his poor assistant... But she honestly wasn't sure if Demetrius would even pay heed to Michael or just start phoning around for a new helper as his current staff lay dying.

The arena was gorgeous, freshly swept, and impeccably maintained. It was surrounded on three sides by seamless mirrors to help riders judge their position and the movements of their mounts. Jumps were set up in the middle. She slowly took in her surroundings, savoring every second she could spend surrounded by splendor.

While Demetrius mounted his own stallion, Bunny stiffened as she remembered that she was wearing a vibrating plug. Apparently, life-or-death situations were also a turn-on for the resident psycho because horseback riding was unsafe at the best of times, let alone when you were playing sick games.

She slid the stirrups down their leathers, measuring them to her arm, then mounted. Bunny was one to land softly on a horse's back, an act of kindness for an animal who did so much for the person sitting astride them. Even so, she could feel the plug push further inside of her, and she bit her lip, stomach tightening.

Demetrius called out to her, "We'll ride for a half hour or so. If you're good, we can go on the trails next time."

She didn't respond, instead letting Maximus walk while her hands slid to the buckle of her reins. This was her element. The buttery leather felt wonderfully pliable in her hands. Bunny's heels were stretched down on instinct, leg long and solid even as it swayed lightly, perfectly in rhythm with the horse's stride.

For the first time in what felt like years, she felt peace settle over her.

After a few passes at an extended walk, she pressed her heels into his sides and sat deep, asking for a trot. He complied immediately and she began rising and falling to his outside leg. Immediately. she regretted it as the plug inside of her woke up. Bunny gasped, faltering and picking up the wrong lead. Her movements became jerky and Maximus answered immediately with a couple of gentle bunny hops. Naturally, he was not the type who would put up with nonsense.

She should have asked for a schoolmaster.

Laughter sounded across the arena and she realized it was two voices, not just one. Bunny shot a venomous glare at Michael, who immediately shut his mouth.

"Come now, Bunny," Demetrius said as he rode up to her on the outside, "I thought you were a better rider than that."

"Fuck you. Eat shit," She growled, curling her upper lip.

"I think the only one who'll be eating shit today is you," He chuckled, eyes heavy with mirth. With that, he cantered off.

"Passing is left shoulder to left shoulder, asshole!" She crowed after him, bristling.

The next thirty minutes passed with the occasional buzz, and Bunny faltering when it happened. She was, for the first time, relieved when the ride ended. Bunny dismounted, landing heavily on the ground and feeling the shock shoot up her legs to her ass, gritting her teeth.

Michael was approaching, already holding Demetrius' horse. He reached his hands out for the reins and she waved him off.

"I take care of my own horses," She said.

"I don't think he's giving you a choice," Michael countered, jerking a thumb over at Demetrius, standing a few feet away. He used a finger to beckon her, and she knew she was to crawl.

In the arena dirt.

Where horses shit and pissed.

Wonderful.

Bunny huffed and dropped to all fours, slowly closing the distance between them.

"Look at you, my sweet Bunny," He said, crouching down and taking her chin in his hand, "You're learning so quickly. Such a smart girl." Bunny set her jaw, skin tingling at the point of contact between her and her captor. It wasn't a pleasant burn.

His face was set into a wicked grin that made her skin crawl. She wasn't sure where this was going, but it couldn't be good.

The mirror, she thought suddenly, *The motherfucker wants to fuck me in front of the mirror.*

"Get undressed, Bunny. Slowly. I want to savor every inch of that beautiful body," Demetrius spoke so softly it was almost a sigh.

Bunny also felt like sighing. And screaming. And crying. Instead, she rose to her knees. Sucking her bottom lip between her teeth nervously, she used shaking hands to unzip her breeches, thumbs pushing them apart to expose naked skin underneath.

She then fell back onto her ass with a decidedly unsexy thud and winced. When she glanced wearily at her captor, he only seemed to be lightly amused at her misstep.

Bunny shed her boots, then the rest of her clothing in slow succession. The cool breeze raised goosebumps along her exposed flesh.

"Run."

His command was growled faintly, wolfish eyes burning with excitement. Bunny stammered for a moment, unsure she had heard him correctly. But she had, and she didn't second guess the opportunity to get the fuck away from this deranged asshole.

Turning on heel, she took off across

the arena, careening toward the tree line that undoubtedly had the trails he had mentioned earlier. Her feet sank into the sand, making for a punishing journey as her calves began to ache from the strain of her movements.

She threw a glance over her shoulder to see Demetrius walking toward her, the distance between them growing as she made it to the grass and pushed faster still.

Running was something she relished. Even given the current circumstances, it provided a feeling of freedom she had been chasing her entire life. Riding horses was a wonderful source of connection and partnership. But running? Every success was entirely her, and something was endlessly satisfying about that.

With each step, Bunny felt herself opening to joy, and the horrors of her most recent days began melting away again. Even as she felt the crisp spring air nipping her most sensitive parts, she couldn't help but fall into the steady rhythm she had grown accustomed to over her years of daily practice in the sport.

Finally, she reached the tree line and stopped to look back.

Demetrius had stopped walking. He was

watching her, face unreadable from the distance between them. The sight of his looming presence snapped her quickly from the trance she had entered and Bunny whipped around to make her way into the woods.

Bunny chose a trail that looked well-worn. It was the least likely to damage her, and she could change direction as she moved further into the woods. With any luck, she'd find a way off the property and safely into a stranger's car.

This was a pipe dream, though. This was obviously a remote location surrounded by a large swath of property. There were likely many miles of meandering trails that connected and diverged repeatedly. However, she was not one to stop believing in the impossible, especially when the sanctity of her body was on the line.

She picked up a steady pace, pulling into form and steeling herself for the rough ground. Her feet were already prickling with pine needles and debris that ground into her soles painfully.

This wouldn't be a pleasant stroll through the woods by any means. But what else could she do? She was losing this battle no matter how she moved the pieces on the board.

Bunny hadn't expected him to chase her

through the woods again. No, she had thought he wanted to watch her face in the mirror of the arena while he buried himself inside of her.

Briefly, she wondered if he'd come faster if she pretended to be in pain while he watched; if he could see her face contort in anguish as he drove his cock as deep as he could force it to go.

Probably, She thought bitterly.

Soft sunlight fell in shimmering streams to the forest floor. The heady scents of dirt and the earliest traces of this season's greenery were thick in the air, comforting even as she felt her feet throb in protest from the harsh terrain. Although she tried to quiet her footsteps, Bunny seemed to crash through the undergrowth, every noise ringing clear through the still air. She winced at every snap and creak.

Chapter Ten

Fear was the largest driving factor in Bunny's life. Past, present, future; she shivered all the same. It was a frigid sort of panic, crashing over her like a sheet of ice. Her shaking hands and dry mouth were the only distractions when she was gripped helplessly in its hold.

It was this emotion that drove her toward success. She feared that she would fail at finding independence above all else, that would become dependent on another human being. Some stayed for companionship, others for finances, and still more for a myriad of other reasons. Bunny had the opposite problem: she *didn't* stay.

Her life was comprised of many lonely years in self-imposed isolation. It was too dangerous to let others inside. What if they didn't like what they found? Regardless of her outer beauty, Bunny often struggled with her lack thereof on the inside. She thought often about her humanity and how much of it she applied or, more importantly, didn't apply to her daily life.

Consistently, she felt that she failed to deliver on the unspoken societal promise to do well by others.

Was she enough? *Could* she be enough?

She decided to be enough for herself, even if that fell short under a different lens. She didn't need another human being to confirm her goodness and she railed against any confirmation given to her. It was nobody's place to judge her, whether positively or otherwise. Taking compliments wasn't her strong suit.

Bunny sighed, head falling forward as she crossed her arms. She had paused to breathe and get her bearings.

She felt terribly exposed; emotionally, rather than physically. While standing there stark naked, Bunny began to shake despite the high-noon sun slipping through the canopy. It wasn't bitterly cold, but there was a subtle chill leftover from the recent winter. The running had kept her warm. Now, the cool was creeping into her skin.

Nearby, she heard rustling. Bunny whipped around, attempting to locate the origin of the sound. She wasn't certain it was him. No, it could have been shifting debris or a small animal. But it wasn't, because not a second later did her captor step out from behind a thick tree.

"Boo," He said, smiling hungrily.

Bunny stepped back, heart picking up an uncomfortable pace. Her melancholic musing was long forgotten as every part of her psyche locked onto the present threat.

"You know, Bunny, you're still the most beautiful fucking thing I've ever seen in my life."

At this, she snarled, teeth bared in a way all too animalistic, "Fuck you."

This outburst earned a hearty laugh, deep and barking. Demetrius then began moving forward, stalking toward her with all the powerful confidence of a jungle animal. He was no longer wearing his riding habit. Bunny briefly realized that she must have been wandering through the woods longer than she thought if he had time to change his clothing and come after her. How long had it been? She had been so lost in her thoughts that she couldn't tell.

He now donned a fully black outfit; shirt, jeans, boots. It made him look less like a leopard and more like a cat burglar. She giggled.

"Something funny, little Bunny?" Demetrius said with a cocked eyebrow.

"Oh, you just look absolutely ridiculous. Sometimes I have to wonder who dresses you and why your taste never evolved past what was obviously a dark, dark time in High School." Immediately, his lips pursed and his eyes narrowed. Bunny gulped while a chill crept along her spine.

And then she turned and ran.

The ruckus behind her made it obvious that he had taken up the chase, and she mentally cursed him for having the advantage of protection in the form of clothing. The ground was battering her already bruised and bleeding feet. Tree branches and bushes snagged at her skin, leaving abrasions in their wake. Bunny could hear him not far behind, but it seemed he was keeping the same pace.

What is he doing? She asked herself, exasperated.

And then she realized that he was running her down like a prey animal. Often in the natural world, predators would give chase and run their victims until ragged. Large herbivores were easier to take down when exhausted.

This went on for what felt like forever. It was a true test of her endurance and she knew she was going to fail. Her heart was hammering at this point, lungs burning. She was losing steam. He was winning.

Finally, her wobbling legs gave out and she fell to her knees, wincing out a yelp as her skin made contact with the rough forest floor.

Her heavy panting nearly covered the noise of his approach. She was close to coughing and choking in desperation for more oxygen. It wasn't a foreign feeling for Bunny. No, she often went as hard as she could while exercising. In this context, it only made her head spin harder while her heart pistoned.

Bunny whimpered in anticipation, pussy beginning to throb even while her brain battled against the purely physiological reaction. He had effectively trained her body to expect sexual gratification whenever he was near.

She didn't like this. She *didn't*.

Demetrius was crouching beside her, his proximity bringing another wave of shivers. "It's okay, Bunny," He murmured, reaching a hand to stroke her cheek with a single finger, "I'm not going to hurt you. Why would I do that? You're mine, and I'm not the type to destroy my toys."

She heaved a gasping, dry sob, empty of tears but painfully filled with overwhelming frustration.

"Come here, Bunny," He whispered, gathering her shaking body into his arms. Demetrius held her to his chest, her head tucked under his chin, hand stroking her hair. At first, Bunny struggled in the embrace but gave up quickly when she realized his iron grip was unrelenting regardless of her efforts.

Bunny instead collapsed in on herself. She had thought she didn't have any more tears to cry, but her body began to dredge up whatever remnants were left.

She choked on her sobs as her life began to slowly unroll in her head like a scroll, revealing scene after scene of horror and heartache. Even while she was brimming with revulsion at his touch, she buried herself into his chest and let herself yield to his embrace.

"I know, sweet one," He whispered, kissing the top of her head, "But you're safe. It doesn't feel like it, but I promise I will protect and adore you for the rest of your life. You will never know another day of fear, sadness, or struggle. As long as you are in my arms, you have nothing to fear in this world. Let yourself accept that, Bunny."

The vibrations in his chest were comforting in the same way as a purr. Bunny was entirely spent, limply holding onto his arms as she caught her breath. Demetrius produced a handkerchief from his pocket, wiping gently at her tears and then pinching her nose.

"Blow."

She did so, briefly disgusted at the concept. He tossed it to the ground.

"What are you going to do to me?" Bunny whispered, lower lip still trembling even as her body began to still. His comforting scent surrounded her.

"I think I'd prefer to keep you guessing. You'll see soon enough."

She didn't respond.

"Hold on a minute," He said, gently releasing her, going slow to ensure her stability.

There was a backpack on the ground that she hadn't realized he had been wearing, likely because it had blended in with the rest of his attire. She assumed he had slipped it off before crouching down next to her.

He took out a blanket, spreading it across

the forest floor, and directed her to lay on her stomach. Bunny obliged.

Demetrius emptied the contents of the bag onto the blanket. She felt his large hand take the base of the plug still lodged in her ass and then whimpered as he pulled it from her. It had been inside of her for too long, making the removal more painful than it should have been.

From there, she heard him unzip his pants and then felt coolness on her ass. He was coating her rear entrance in lube, a finger slipping in, and then two. Bunny mewled, tensing and releasing as he began to twist and thrust, readying her so that she could take his cock.

After working her thoroughly, Demetrius positioned himself and leaned his head down so that his mouth was level with her ear. "Relax and take it for me like a good girl."

His whisper sent electricity surging through her body and into her groin. She groaned, pressing her face into the blanket.

With that, she felt the head of his manhood press against her rear entrance and then slowly inside of her. Bunny let loose an inhuman sound, somewhere between a throaty moan and gargle.

Demetrius was slow and gentle, pushing further inside of her with every measured thrust. The friction built, pleasure slowly following as he found the spot inside of her that made her vision blur. Bunny's hips began to wave back and forth, encouraging him deeper. She let go of the fear, let loose the heavy burden weighing on her since long before her kidnapping.

At this moment, she only allowed herself to feel the intense fullness bringing her otherworldly pleasure.

"That's my girl, Bunny. God, you feel incredible," Demetrius panted, quaking as he paced himself. Bunny whined and began pushing backward into his driving hips. They found a perfect rhythm, grinding against each other.

Heat was building from a crackle to a bonfire in her belly. Bunny's sides heaved as the desire to climax spiraled into an immediate need.

But she did her best to hold herself back, refusing to ask this psychotic man for his permission to ascend that peak. That humiliation was a step too far for this moment, while he was already degrading her so thoroughly.

And then his hands were searching under her stomach, reaching downward. Bunny gasped as his fingers found her clit and began circling the throbbing bud. Her moans became desperate, the dual stimulation pulling her closer to the edge. His fingers worked her clit mercilessly.

She felt so blissfully full, his cock stretching her to what she assumed had to be her limit. And the friction, the spot he was hitting; the desire for climax would not stop building. It roared in her, a primal call she couldn't ignore. Bunny gasped out, "Please, can I… Can I… come?" The last word was spat out as quickly as she could manage.

"Yes, Bunny," Demetrius moaned, "Come for me, baby."

Bunny felt the mounting peaks come closer together, pussy contracting with each pulse of pleasure. Within seconds, she was tumbling over the edge into a prismatic world of color and light. She squeezed her eyes shut, mouth open.

Demetrius let loose a thunderous groan at the same time, hips jerking erratically as his own orgasm took him.

They both collapsed, his body pressing her into the blanket in a way that was not unpleasant. In fact, the weight was almost comforting She didn't know how long they lay there before

Demetrius broke the silence.

"Let's get you cleaned up, my love," He said, pulling himself out of her and kneeling between her legs.

Demetrius proceeded to use baby wipes everywhere that lube left her covered in a sticky, slick film. He was slow and thorough and, surprisingly, she didn't feel filthy from his touch.

The trip back was quiet. Bunny was too tired to speak after the chase and her orgasm. Demetrius seemed at peace in the silence, the occasional birdsong breaking it.

She stumbled her way into the car once they were back. To her surprise, he allowed her into the backseat, sitting down and pulling her head into his lap. She didn't fight him, and soon she fell fast asleep.

Chapter Eleven

Bunny spent the rest of the afternoon into evening curled in the safety of her blanket. Her entire body was sore. She was devoid of strength mentally, physically, and emotionally.

What did he mean in the forest? That he would protect her? Keep her safe?

There was no guarantee of safety in this life. That much she had learned early and often. Anybody attempting to sell you steadfast security was peddling a pipe dream for the feckless.

No, Bunny knew all too well the crushing reality that terrible things happened… and they did so consistently. She wouldn't be lulled by a false sense of protection offered by a man she hated. Even if he could offer her the safety he promised, it came at a terrible price she was unwilling to pay. She would be forced out into the open, left completely vulnerable.

Bunny had a feeling, however, that he was the type who could manage to squeeze blood from a stone. She could resist him with everything she had. In the end, it wouldn't make a difference to her situation.

The tenderness in her feet had worsened as bruises bloomed and they began to itch and burn from the abrasions she had amassed.

Of course, she could rummage through the bathroom and perhaps find first aid supplies, but she couldn't bring herself to move. It wasn't the usual state of depression or despair keeping her cemented to the floor.

Bunny was just so bone tired.

Curling into a tighter ball, she squeezed her eyes shut and whimpered as her body ached in protest. Even with the pain, all she could think about was his strong arms wrapped around her as she cried helplessly into his chest.

The memory *burned*.

Continued nudity was one thing, as was the degrading sex. To Bunny, emotional nakedness was so much worse. There was a difference between the body and soul. One you simply inhabited, and the other was your entirety.

A knock sounded in the silence, and she

sucked in a startled breath. Demetrius walked in, closing the door softly behind him, and turned to look at her. It was a good few seconds before he began to speak.

"I came to tend to you, little Bunny."

She retreated further into her nest. The last thing she wanted was for this deranged man to put his hands on her again, especially if it ended similarly to how it had before. Even with her obvious discomfort, he strode forward until he was at the edge of her sleeping pad.

"Come to me, Bunny," Demetrius said softly, kneeling and holding his hands out. Bunny knew better than to refuse him.

She let the blanket fall around her and crawled over, refusing to make eye contact.

"There's my good girl," He purred, pulling her into his chest and kissing the crown of her head. Bunny stiffened. Although she was loathe to admit it, there was a certain security in being held by a large, strong man who smelled intoxicatingly good. Even if he was also actively tormenting you for fun.

Demetrius said nothing. Instead, he stroked her hair and caressed her cheek with a touch gentler than he should have been capable of. He lifted her, carrying her bridal style toward the bathroom. Bunny sighed and let her head fall over, resting against him. She was so tired that she could barely keep her eyes open, and he was so warm and smelled so good.

Once inside, he laid her in the tub and turned on the faucet, sitting on the edge and feeling the water as it poured out. Once satisfied with the temperature, he poured in Epsom salts and bubble bath.

He did not move to disrobe.

Bunny would have commented but the words wouldn't seem to form. Her head was swimming. She ran her fingers through the water, feeling it whirl around her open fingers. Her eyes fluttered, and she decided to close them in favor of focusing on her moving hands.

Demetrius returned with a washcloth and rolled-up sleeves. She only opened an eye to look at him briefly. He reached over to gently hold her face, turning her head toward him. "I'm going to make you feel better, baby. I know today was a lot for you. You did so good for me, though. You deserve to be taken care of."

Bunny let her head lay limp in his hand, releasing a soft noise of acknowledgment.

He poured a generous amount of soap into the washcloth and began gently wiping down her arms and chest, softly circling her nipples until Bunny moaned. His touch was delicate and petal soft. This was nothing like the steel-hard presence he had previously. No, she was getting a look at a different side of the man, one she wasn't sure she wanted to see.

If her captor was kind, it would make it that much harder for her to hate him entirely. The last thing Bunny wanted was to develop some fucked up trauma bond to this man.

"Stand up, Bunny."

She whimpered, "I don't think I can."

Demetrius chuckled as though pleased with the results of his earlier handiwork.

"That's okay. Hold onto me, then, baby." He held out an arm for her to stabilize herself. Bunny put both of her arms over his and leaned heavily on him. She felt precarious, hanging from him with little energy to right herself if her grip became slack. Demetrius slowly stood, putting his other hand on the small of her back.

"Let's get you showered, sweet Bunny," he whispered tenderly. It was true that she needed to stand under the spray; she could feel sheets of suds slipping down her body as she stood on wobbling legs.

Demetrius ensured Bunny was stable on her feet and then let go of her. Beginning to undress, he raked his eyes slowly over her body. She shuddered despite the heady steam swirling around. She didn't think she could take him.

Even if Bunny hated the man to his rotten core, she couldn't help but admire his physique. Demetrius rippled with muscle through every movement. And, as her own eyes drifted south, he had a cock to be admired. It was girthy and easily over eight inches, with a slight curve towards himself when it was fully hard.

It struck Bunny as fitting that even his dick seemed to bend to his will.

Demetrius stepped over the tub lip. He didn't slosh a single drop of water as he moved toward the drain, flipping the switch. Turning back toward Bunny, he again collected her in his arms and held her close. She was too spent to fight and leaned into him wearily.

They stood there in a tight embrace as the water level slowly lowered.

Demetrius turned the showerhead on, blasting them with water cold enough to shock her system.

"What the FUCK?" She shrieked, suddenly finding the strength to jump out of the way of the spray.

"Come on, Bunny, it's good for you," Demetrius crowed, grabbing her into a bear hug. She kicked viciously, leaning her head down to bite down on his arm. He didn't seem to mind at all, howling in laughter from the horrified noises and hateful curses leaving her mouth.

The water slowly warmed and Bunny stopped fighting, panting with the effort of trying to get away. She could taste copper and she knew she had broken skin when she bit him.

It served him right.

"What the fuck is your pro-" Her snarl was cut short by his lips on hers. Demetrius charged forward, pressing her hard into the wall. They were still well within range of the now thankfully warm water, filling the already balmy air with thick rivulets of steam.

She gasped in shock, mouth opening to his, and Demetrius took full advantage. His tongue gently explored her mouth while his hands gripped her hips. Bunny whimpered, eyes rolling as he ground his hard cock into her center, solidifying his intent.

He wanted her again.

Bunny knew that fighting him would only end in tragedy for her. So, she gave in, kissing him back fiercely and lifting a knee to hook his hip. She pulled him closer and his hand came down to cup the underside of her knee, encouraging her leg to hitch up higher.

Her arms were now wrapped around his neck as they moved their mouths in a rhythm normally formed by longtime partners.

Demetrius broke the kiss, leaning his head forward so he could whisper into her ear, "Well, that certainly woke you from your little pity party, didn't it?"

"You're an ass," She hissed, tensing in fury as she remembered the stunt he had pulled not even a few minutes ago.

"You are what you eat," He chuckled, provoking an indignant cry from her, but his lips covered hers before she could offer any rebuttal.

Pressing her back into the wall, Demetrius bent slightly and lifted her by the backs of her knees so her pussy was bared to him, while her back was stabilized on the shower wall.

"Demetrius, I'm going to fall," She said,

voice wavering as she wrapped her arms around his neck for security.

"Only if I decide to drop you, so think twice about being naughty."

He had her effectively pinned and even though she wriggled hard, she couldn't get away from the incredible crush of his hips.

And then, to her horror, he released a leg to slip his hand between them. As he found her clit, she wrapped that leg around his waist in a desperate bid to find security. The fall would hurt, and he'd likely have a punishment planned. Demetrius used two fingers to lightly pinch and squeeze her clit and then began circling it with his thumb. He switched between these two movements as his mouth explored the expanse of her neck. She could feel teeth and tongue and lips, and a fire was building deep in her belly while his hand played the perfect rhythm to bring her to climax.

"Are- are you going to fuck me?" She managed to say, wondering when her throbbing pussy would once more be filled. In this state, she didn't think; she *knew* it would hurt.

"No, Bunny. This isn't about me. This is only about you, baby. You might not believe me but I live only to worship you."

In an instant, Bunny felt herself in free fall. She cried out. Her eyes were wide but unseeing as her world exploded into a kaleidoscope of color and brightness. This was the pinnacle of pleasure. It was like a never-ending orgasm, back-to-back waves making the muscles in her pussy clench powerfully.

He paused, panting in her ear to say, "What a naughty girl, Bunny. I don't think you asked permission before you came, did you?"

The rest of the shower went smoothly. He insisted on washing her body, telling her he needed to take responsibility for his pretty, little pet. Bunny retorted that people who fucked their pets belonged in prison, earning a hard smack on her ass. He had also put her collar back on once she was dry enough, telling her, "We wouldn't want you to forget who you belong to."

Bunny was too tired at that point to even say anything. Perhaps this was it; he was breaking her down, bit by bit. She knew his ultimate goal was to dampen her spirit and bring her to heel.

To her disgust, it might be working.

The bed beneath her felt blissfully soft. Demetrius had laid her down gently on it before walking to the bathroom and back. He held a couple of bottles and a box of bandages.

Once he had made his way back over, he put everything on the bedside table. Bunny eyed everything suspiciously. She didn't trust him.

He started with her feet. She hadn't noticed the tiny squeezable bottle of antibacterial ointment, but she was grateful for it as soon as he sat down and began applying it to the scrapes. Demetrius' touch was light but thoroughly ensured every scratch was satisfactorily tended.

Next, he picked up a bottle of massage oil. Bunny perked up at that and then deflated. *Is he going to make me give him a fucking massage?* The thought was bitter and suspicious, but she couldn't be blamed for being wary of his often dubious intentions.

Instead of asking her to rub him down, he poured a cold trail down her spine, and she squirmed in response. He smiled.

Demetrius obviously knew what he was doing, and Bunny quickly found herself moaning into the bed as he worked her tight muscles. He was gentle in deference to her already aching body. This went on for what seemed far too long but was also far too short a time. He covered her entire body, leaving no inch untouched by his kneading hands. Once he was done, he kissed her temple and whispered, "Rest now, Bunny. We'll play again later tonight for dinner."

Chapter Twelve

Bunny woke up to a booming knock. She sleepily raised her head just in time to see Michael pop his head into the room.

"I figured you'd probably be late if I didn't wake you up. God knows I have enough to do and now I have to watch out for your dumbass, too." He grumbled, doing his best to look away from her naked form.

"Maybe if you were better at your job it wouldn't be so hard to do it," Bunny said languidly, stretching slowly out, baring herself to him entirely.

"Well, you've certainly gotten comfortable in… What? How long has it even been? Feels like fucking forever with the trouble you always seem to be causing."

"Look, Michael, I don't have time for this, alright? I have a dinner date with a sadist to attend and you're holding me up. Besides, if this is my life now, I'd better make the best of it." Her tone was bitter.

He looked at her, bewildered by her nonchalance but catching onto her dismissal.

"Alright, whatever. Just don't be late."

With that, Michael was gone.

Bunny stood, taking stock of her body. She felt far better after he had bathed and massaged her. What could he have planned? Surely it was a punishment of some sort, but one involving food? She decided against thinking about it more. Anticipation was half of the torture associated with her perceived wrongdoings.

Besides, it reminded her that she now had to ask before allowing herself the simple pleasure of an orgasm.

Bunny finally left the room, padding down the hallway and eventually into the dining area off the side of the kitchen. The room was narrow and long, filled with an impressive table lined by understated but ornate chairs.

She sauntered toward Demetrius, heading to the chair next to this, where she assumed he would want her to sit.

"No."

His voice echoed through the room, and Bunny looked at him quizzically. Demetrius then pointed to the floor a few feet away from him.

There was a fucking dog bowl.

Bunny's jaw dropped. She crossed her arms and looked at him, face set with rage.

"Absolutely the fuck not."

"Are you sure? Because I think I can convince you, and I don't think you want me to."

She bared her teeth at him with a curled lip and eyes that shone. Her anger was reaching a boiling point and she wasn't sure how much longer she could go without taking a swing at this stupid, smug face.

"Easy way, or hard way, Bunny?" Demetrius asked, sounding bored as he shook out a cloth napkin before settling it in his lap.

Suddenly, the fight was gone, and Bunny walked over to the dog bowl. She sank to her knees, tears pricking at the corners of her eyes. Her hair fell in limp strands, still wet.

She heard movement behind her and suddenly Demetrius was behind her, gathering her hair into his hands. He then tied it back with… something. It wasn't a hair tie. Out of the corner of her eye, she saw the end of a ribbon.

"I don't want to have to bathe you again today," He chuckled, reaching down to gently massage one of her breasts. The lack of her response inspired him to begin toying gently with the nipple, rubbing and tweaking the peak.

Bunny whimpered pathetically as the rosy buds tightened and hardened under his touch. "Good girl," He said.

Bunny started at the sound of foreign voices, head whipping around just in time to see two men walk into the room. They looked strikingly similar to Demetrius in stature and dress, but one was a blonde and the other had hair the color of fresh tobacco.

She began hyperventilating. Her nudity became something glaringly obvious to her... and this new audience. Both men stared her down as though she were prey beneath their paws. There was an undeniable hunger in their fixation on her naked body.

Demetrius was still kneeling next to her. He began to pet her hair softly, ignoring the wetness on his hands from the still-damp strands.

"Bunny, you're okay. I promise," He leaned down to whisper in her ear, "You're going to make me and my associates very happy tonight. Just be a good girl and do as you're told. Otherwise, you'll have to deal with three wicked minds dreaming up your punishment."

She sucked in a breath. Bunny wasn't sure where this was headed, and she could feel fear beginning to swell in her abdomen. If she was lucky, they were there to humiliate her as they ate. If she wasn't…

She didn't want to think of it further. Bunny wouldn't give Demetrius the satisfaction of her anticipation. She was convinced that was half of what he got off on. Instead, Bunny bolstered herself with the thought of her warm, thick blanket, and how she would curl up in it once she was put back in her metaphorical cage.

The men sat down and began a light conversation with Demetrius. It was almost as though she was forgotten as quickly as she was visually devoured. They weren't paying her any mind at all. Not that she really cared, of course, but part of her was a little insulted that they could concentrate on anything but the naked woman in front of them.

Self-control was obviously something they all had in spades. It was unsurprising to her. Birds of a feather flocked together. She was fighting the urge to roll her eyes.

Michael suddenly appeared with a cart, setting a plate in front of each man. He was red-faced and clearing his throat from time to time. When it was time to serve Bunny, he picked up a bowl from the cart and dumped its contents into her bowl. It was a mixture of cut-up steak, she assumed the same filet the others were enjoying, and an assortment of roasted vegetables.

"Who let the dogs out, am I right?" Michael murmured when he was crouched next to her.

"Fuck you, Michael. I'll kill you." She hissed out of the corner of her mouth.

And then he was gone. It was just her, a dog bowl, and predatory men staring her down with hawkish eyes. Demetrius cleared his throat and she took that as her cue. Bunny lowered her head and began to tenderly eat pieces of meat as neatly as possible.

It was delicious. It was the best filet she had ever had. Perfectly seared, seasoned, and coated in what tasted like a garlic butter sauce. Too bad she was being thoroughly and publicly humiliated as she ate, turning every bite into torture as she realized that, despite her efforts, the juices were collecting on her jaw and cheeks.

"Who's a good girl?" One of the men called out, she wasn't sure which, as though urging on a dog. All three laughed boisterously. Before she could stop herself, in a fit of rage and hatred, Bunny snapped back.

"Fuck you, asshole."

And then there was silence until Demetrius broke it.

"Well, gentlemen, I think I'm satisfied with dinner. What do you say we get ready for dessert?"

They both heartily agreed and she heard the sliding of chairs. Bunny's heart pounded in her chest, knowing she had thoroughly fucked up.

Three wicked minds, She remembered his words in a panic, *What have I done?*

The sound of Demetrius approaching ignited shivers down her quickly dissolving spine. Bunny did not feel brave anymore.

He knelt and wrapped a hand around her throat, pulling her backward into his chest. "Look at my messy girl," Demetrius crooned in a cloying tone, "Let's take care of that," He began gently wiping her face with a wet napkin.

Bunny was frozen, chest sticking out, the

front of her body fully on display. One of the other men, the blonde, approached. He knelt and grinned savagely at her before leaning his head down to capture a nipple between his lips.

Demetrius held her there, hand tightening before she felt his other hand slip between her legs after her face was clean. The other man was suddenly beside her, taking the other breast into his warm, wet mouth. She gasped, the three points of stimulation sending searing pleasure pounding deep in her pussy.

His hand worked her relentlessly. He had found her clit and was rubbing a finger around it.

Bunny's hips began to buck against her will, gasps escaping her open mouth. "No, no, no," She groaned, wriggling under the strain of her mounting orgasm.

"Yes, yes, yes," Demetrius replied diabolically.

All three stopped. The two new men leaned away from her, getting off the floor and dusting their pants with their hands.

"Well, that was fun," The blonde said, "Let's continue to the lounge. I'm excited for the party to begin." It was infuriatingly casual. Everything was. They went from assaulting her to preparing for a casual get together.

"Let's," Demetrius responded, clapping his hands together, "Just let me gather up my pet and I'll be right in. I assume you remember the way…?"

"Of course, Demetrius. We'll be waiting," The tobacco-haired man finally spoke, his voice soft and cold as snow. If she wasn't already chilled to the bone, it would have been enough to turn her blood to ice.

Once they left the room Demetrius pulled her up by her neck. To her surprise, he spun her around and pulled her into his chest, wrapping his arms around her shoulders and back.

"Such a spitfire, little Bunny," He said into her hair, "You made my hands wet, you know."

"That happens when you touch hair that's been in a shower," She responded dryly.

"Oh, I was talking about that pretty little pussy of yours," He punctuated the end of the sentence by moving a hand to his face and running his tongue slowly up a finger, eyes locked onto hers, "You have no idea how good you taste."

Bunny felt heat growing, turning into a molten coil in her belly. She didn't want to want him, but what choice did she have?

She had been stuck here for long enough that it was highly unlikely she could ever hope for rescue. That meant that she had to rely on herself to escape. Unfortunately, she was quickly losing motivation.

Demetrius held her tightly for a few moments, breathing her in, and nuzzling the top of her head.

What the fuck is he doing? She thought, simultaneously repulsed by his affections and attracted by them. The lack of human contact outside interactions with Demetrius and Michael was clearly wearing on her.

Then, he turned, bringing her with him. She ended up beside him, his arm around her waist, and they walked in step toward the study.

The two men had made themselves comfortable, sipping scotch poured over ice. Their ties were undone and they were lounging like lazy cats over their respective chairs.

But that wasn't what Bunny noticed first.

An assortment of toys were laid on the

floor across a blanket. Bunny immediately froze, digging her heels into the ground, and whimpered, "No, please, I don't want to."

Demetrius heaved a sigh, scooping her up and walking over to an empty chair. She wound up curled in his lap face pressed into his chest, chilled by the realization that she would have to perform for the entire group.

"Settle down, Bunny," Demetrius said warmly, tightening his grip around her, "You're going to be wonderful. Everybody is here to see this beautiful body on display."

"I don't want to be on display," She cried out so softly she wasn't sure he heard her.

"Oh, but you will. For you, the attention will be addictive, you vain little slut." It wasn't unkind how he said it, but she took offense to the final word all the same.

With that, Demetrius cleared his throat and addressed the two men. They began chatting about things Bunny knew nothing about; stocks, bonds, business deals. It was horribly boring and she felt herself drifting once or twice, despite her growing dread.

It didn't help that Demetrius was tracing circles on her back, stroking her hair, treating her so tenderly even as he conspired to humiliate her.

A kiss was pressed to her forehead before he whispered, "I think it's time for the show, Bunny." She gulped as he slid her off his lap, standing on shaking legs, unsure of what to do.

"On the blanket, little Bunny," Demetrius said, sounding bored suddenly.

Without making eye contact with any of the men, who were unbuckling their pants, she shuffled to the blanket and kneeled on it. There were several toys, all varying in size and usage. She picked up a small butt plug.

"I think something bigger is more suiting," Tobacco-hair mused, "After all, you're going to have my cock in that tight ass tonight."

Bunny glanced up and felt her face flush deeply when she noticed the aforementioned cock out and on full display. It was around the same size as Demetrius', thick and full. The bulbous head was already purple.

She set the toy back down and picked one about the size of her fist. The budding nervousness muddled with her fear, creating a mixture of emotions that made her stomach roil.

They all sat in silence, the blonde slowly stroking his dick, the other two watching expectantly. She wasn't sure how they could be so comfortable with one another. It seemed odd to her that they would be so open with their pleasure. Bunny was certain they had done this together before. She wondered if it was another kidnapping victim or a willing participant.

"Turn around, Bunny. Face down, ass up."

It was tobacco-hair. She set her jaw, slowly doing as he asked, face burning. Bunny wasn't sure if she wanted to cry or throw up, but she was determined to do neither. She wouldn't give them the satisfaction of knowing they had broken her so completely.

Generously coating her fingers with lube, she reached between her legs and found her tight entrance, rubbing it gently. The angle was awkward but workable and soon she was pressing past her ring of muscle, whimpering as she readied herself.

"That's my good girl," Demetrius whispered so quietly that it would have gone unheard if not for the room's silence. The only sounds were panting men and her own whimpers.

Satisfied with her readiness, and desperate for the show to end, Bunny poured lube on the toy. She positioned it and began rocking it back and forth until it was lodged inside of her. She gasped, flexing from the fullness she felt immediately.

"Pleasure yourself. Use the vibrator on your clit. Don't take it off until you're told to. You don't have permission to come," Demetrius spoke again, calling out his commands loudly.

She shifted onto her back, spreading her legs wide, gripping the vibrator. Her glistening pussy was finally fully unveiled to her viewers. Even while she felt terribly dirty, her body was responding in full.

Demetrius was right. She was an attention whore, and a deep, dark part of her relished in the hungry gazes trained on her.

As she punched the vibrator to a low setting, she began to feel herself disassociate. She felt as though she were floating in the open air, like nothing around her was real. It made this humiliating exhibition feel more tolerable.

Bunny pressed the toy to her swollen clit, mewling at the way the buzzing bathed her belly in a wondrous warmth. Her fuzzy head swam as she disconnected from her body. All she could feel now was a sinful lust and the satisfaction of giving her body what it craved.

But as the pressure built, she began wriggling, desperate to break contact with the powerful toy. Even at the lowest setting, it was enough to rock her.

"Higher, Bunny."

She cried out, "Please, no, please," but did as she was told. Bunny started stammering, pleading, begging. She was babbling incoherently as her body shook and her hips thrashed. She kept the vibrator firmly in place even while her body fought desperately to get away from it.

"That's enough," Demetrius said, apparently satisfied with her display. Bunny immediately turned the vibrator off. She was simultaneously relieved and terrified. She gasped and panted, face flushed. Her pussy was throbbing, body crying out for release.

Demetrius beckoned her with a finger. Walking over to him with an awkward gait, still getting used to the plug deep inside of her, Bunny noticed he had procured a pill. He patted his lap and Bunny slid into it, curling into him. Even while she did her best to keep a distance, she found Demetrius' arms to be a safe place.

She could feel how the trauma she was enduring was binding her to him. He would take her to the brink, torturing her body with unbearable pleasure, and then hold her once he had successfully destroyed. It was inevitable that she'd find comfort in him.

He was also a familiar place to harbor from the storm she was surrounded by. Better the devil she knew than the devils she didn't.

He pinched the pill between two fingers, bringing it to her lips. "This is going to help you relax, Bunny. It's just a Xanax."

Just a Xanax, my ass, She thought bitterly. Bunny had been prescribed the medication before for extreme anxiety, one of many Benzos she had tried over the years. She knew she would be on her ass within minutes once she ingested the white disc.

So, she did exactly that without complaint with a sip of bitter scotch that bit her tongue and burned her throat on the way down.

He held her close, tucking her head under his chin, and rubbing her back. His silky clothing felt like heaven against her skin. Bunny snuggled in closer, sighing gently as the Xanax began to work. In a few minutes, she was floating.

Between the dissociation and the medication, Bunny began to feel an incredible relaxation settle across her body. She stretched out, legs drooping over one arm of the chair while her head hung from the other side. Bunny let her arms fall to either side, one curled against Demetrius, the other dangling.

"I think she's ready, gentlemen," Her captor said with a hearty laugh, taking a nipple between his fingers. Bunny squirmed under his touch, moaning softly.

Suddenly for her, everything meant nothing. She didn't care at all about the men surrounding her or their intentions. It was a world of softness and pleasure, and, to her surprise, she wanted to be touched.

More hands began roaming her body, a mouth taking the other nipple, tongue swirling around the tender peak. Her clit was being circled by yet another hand, and then her lips were captured by Demetrius. She kissed him back in earnest, tongue pressing for entry that was quickly granted.

Demetrius paused momentarily, as though surprised, and then took full advantage of her state. The two assailants groped her body as she and Demetrius explored each other's mouths. He sucked on her tongue, and she moaned breathlessly as lust consumed her.

Demetrius shooed the other men away, standing up and holding Bunny so she leaned against him. "Now, I know we're all desperate to get to the meat of the matter," Demetrius slapped her ass, earning a chuckle from the other two and a yelp from her, "But I think we all also remember the mishap at dinner."

Her heart dropped.

Shit.

"Come along, Bunny," He said, walking her over to the chaise lounge where he had punished her previously. She attempted to stop, her movements uncoordinated and slow, but Demetrius picked her up.

When he sat on the couch, still cradling her, he leaned his head down and rubbed his nose against hers. She swallowed hard.

"You couldn't have thought we'd let you get away with that, could you?" He murmured, a finger tracing her jawline, "Now, turn over, naughty girl."

Bunny felt her eyes fill with tears, and something flickered in Demetrius' expression. It was something like hesitation. But she didn't have time to think about it because she was obeying him almost without thought, and suddenly he was rubbing her ass with a large, strong hand. The plug moved as he tugged at it, earning a small, pitiful noise from Bunny.

"Please don't do this," Her voice was slurred, the drug making it hard for her to think.

"You know I have to, Bunny." His voice was steely, set with determination. There wasn't a hint of promise to hold back in his tone, regardless of the look in his eyes.

Demetrius landed the first hit softly. After that, he picked up the pace, spanking her viciously, as though angry that he had to in the first place. Bunny laid still through the punishment. She didn't have the energy to move and it didn't hurt so much in her current state. She just felt hopelessly helpless and entirely at his mercy, and hated it. But there was something almost pleasing to the feeling of his hand landing blow after blow.

She squeezed her legs together in an effort to find stimulation, moaning despite herself. Once it was over, Demetrius was panting with the expended effort, and she was sure her ass would be bruised from the treatment.

And the night was long from over.

Chapter Thirteen

The room didn't spin so much as it wavered. Bunny felt soft. There was no other way to explain it. Every movement was pleasant and she felt entirely at peace.

She realized she was still draped over his lap. Her tears were dried but her face was stained. That was okay. She figured the lunatics doing this to her would harden at the sight of it.

Demetrius pushed her off of him but caught her before she could fall.

"Steady now, Bunny," He said, letting her hold onto one of his forearms. She looked at him and smiled, dazed and filled with an overwhelming sense of peace. Demetrius looked at her with wonderment, as though he had never seen a smile thrown his way before. He seemed as dazed as she was.

"I would hate to break up your little

moment, but we have urgent business to attend to," The blonde said, hand clasping his hardened cock. He was covered in a sheen of sweat, eyes glazed as he took in Bunny, naked but for the collar around her elegant neck.

Demetrius hummed thoughtfully, leading Bunny toward the men.

"Shall we, gentlemen?" He said, Bunny still holding his forearm for dear life.

He knelt to the ground, bringing her with him, and the other two men began to undress. "I'm going to watch first, okay? Be a good girl for them. I know it's going to be hard, but you can do this for me." He tucked her hair behind her ear and she leaned into his touch, barely registering his voice.

The blond replaced Demetrius, hand wrapping gently around the back of her neck and positioning his cock at her mouth. She opened it, doing her best to take his entire length, but choking helplessly as he began to thrust his hips.

"That's it, Bunny, just like that," The tobacco-haired man was whispering to her, his free hand moving between her legs to work her swelling clit. Bunny moaned around the thick cock filling her mouth and stretching down into her throat.

Her arms hung listlessly at her sides. She was still floating somewhere far away, entirely comfortable in her numbness. It made him fucking her face that much more bearable. Enjoyable, even.

Suddenly, her mouth was empty, and she turned her head. He was now standing, manhood presented. Instead of being pressed to it, Bunny leaned forward and took it into her mouth, sucking as she bobbed her head.

He leaned his head back and groaned, "Oh my God. Fuck."
Out of the corner of her eye, she saw Demetrius. He was watching intently. The scotch glass he was swirling was half-empty.

"As much as I love fucking that pretty face, I can't wait anymore. I need to feel your tight pussy around my cock. I'm going to make you come so hard that you cry," The man of few words with tobacco-colored hair finally said more than a sentence, and she shuddered.

They were both kneeling now, one in front of her, one behind. The plug inside of her was gently pulled out, replaced quickly by the tip of the blonde's cock. He began gently moving his hips back and forth, swaying them so that he could gain access as he gripped her hips to help keep her in position.

When he filled her, she felt a long, throaty moan falling from her lips. She was so *full*.

It wasn't enough, though. It wasn't enough. She needed more. In this condition, she had no shame, no guilt, no reservation. She wanted that tobacco-haired man to bury himself up to the hilt in her aching cunt.

Moments later, as though bidden by her thoughts alone, he did exactly that. The man went blissfully slow, gently filling her until she was frozen from the feeling. It was as though a single movement could rip her in two. Both men were panting in her ears, and then she felt hands, she wasn't sure whose, playing with her nipples.

Another set of hands gripped her hips and began rocking them, lifting her up and down so she was being fucked by both men simultaneously.

Nirvana wouldn't do the feeling justice. Bunny was sure her moaning could be heard down the hall. Her throat was practically raw from the mewling and whining she now had no control over. She felt the two men lock lips next to her head, and heard the tell-tale sounds of mouths exploring each other.

Oh, God, holy shit, she thought as she listened to them make out, even her thoughts slurred. She couldn't help but feel another wave of lust settle over her. It was just so goddamn hot.

The tobacco-haired man turned his head and captured her lips in his, while the blonde nibbled on her earlobe. The pair continued to switch between making out with each other, switching to Bunny, while exploring all three bodies with their hands.

Demetrius had stood up, setting his now empty glass down, and stumbled over to her. His cock had fallen to half-mast but was quickly swelling again with her hot breath clouding around it as she puffed with the effort of taking both cocks at once.

"Suck." His command rang out among the groans and grunts of the other two men, and she complied immediately, attracted to the idea of yet more stimulation.

He tasted slightly salty, precum having beaded at the peak of his manhood.
She rocked her head back and forth, working hard to take him further and further until he was

practically down her throat.

Bunny was spiraling rapidly, vibrating with the pleasure that was now explosive in her belly. She pulled her mouth from his cock and looked up at him, spit forming a string between the tip and her lips.

"Can I come?" She wailed, overcome with the potent rapture that was breaking through the drug-induced haze.

Demetrius stared down at her, eyes shining with a lust she had not seen in them before, "Yes," he grabbed her chin and continued, "But don't you dare look away from me while you do."

Bunny was sent flying over the edge into a brilliant nothingness. The room dissolved around her and she could only see Demetrius; his parted lips, his lupine eyes. His ravenous expression deepened as he visually devoured her while she came. She locked onto his gaze even as everything else was lost to sight, mouth open and eyes widening to saucers.

It was like nothing she had ever felt. She was so full, and two sets of hands were caressing and pinching and gently circling in all the right places. In this pleasure that stole nearly all her senses, Bunny could hardly hear the men around her all finding their climax in unison.

She realized she was suddenly sobbing, almost hysterically, as the other two pulled out of her. Demetrius quickly drew her to his chest, rocking her back and forth. Bunny balled herself up in his lap. He peppered gentle kisses across her forehead, her cheeks, her nose.

"Bunny, love, you're okay," He whispered as he tightened his hold, hushing and soothing her as she continued to cry uncontrollably.

Snot bubbled from her nose and Demetrius grabbed a shirt from next to him, wiping away the nastiness as it dripped.

"Hey, what the fuck? That's my shirt!" One of the men exclaimed.

"Find a different one. Get out," Demetrius hissed, and Bunny briefly questioned his tone. He seemed in a bad mood for somebody who had likely just finished fulfilling one of his darkest fantasies.

She couldn't make herself care, though. She only wanted to curl closer to him, holding onto his arm with a tightly gripped hand, desperate for contact.

"Oh, my Bunny," He whispered, nuzzling her face, "My darling girl. Let's clean you up."

He had carried her bridal style to the bathroom once again. It was becoming a habit she was sure would become set in stone as the days passed, and those days would turn into weeks. But would they turn to months? Years? How long was he planning on keeping her? And what was his plan if he grew tired of using her as his fuck toy?

Bunny banished the train of thought. So far, he seemed rather fond of her, and she was beginning to feel the stirrings of attachment somewhere deep inside of herself.

Demetrius laid her down on the floor and began readying a bath. He had dressed in plaid pajama bottoms and a black shirt that clung to his muscular body. In her altered state, Bunny could only think of what a mouthwatering man he was.

The cool tiles felt refreshing against her hot skin. She could feel the ache between her legs building as she shifted to expose more skin to the floor. Her thighs were sticky with the come of the men who had used her freely just moments before. It leaked steadily from both holes.

Demetrius was back, lifting her and lowering her into the steaming water. As she lay soaking, he placed a bath bomb in the water. "Mmmmm," Bunny was still feeling the effects of the Xanax, the bath adding a new layer of weightlessness to her already floating body. It felt incredible. This was possibly the happiest moment of her life. Although, that was likely the Xanax speaking.

Demetrius sighed, pushing her hair back, and gently cleaning her face with a washcloth. It was wonderfully soft and she relished in the feeling of being taken care of. She felt like a small child again, but instead of bruises and screaming, she was enjoying the tender care that she should have been afforded to her all along.

Demetrius continued wiping her body down, paying extra attention between her legs to wash away the thick liquid coating her.

"Why are you being so kind to me?" She whispered, looking at him from under her thick lashes, eyelids drooping with fatigue.

"Because you deserve it, my love," He whispered back, cupping her face and rubbing his thumb along the apple of her cheek. His words made her eyes brim with tears again, and she let loose a choking sob, suddenly overcome with grief; for her childhood, for her current situation, for all the brokenness inside of her that she refused to face.

Demetrius drained the tub while she wept loudly into the side of it. He turned on the shower and quickly stood her up, the water soaking him as he worked to wash the suds from her body. Once satisfied that she was clean, he turned off the spray, then wrapped her in a steaming, fluffy towel pulled from the warmer next to the shower.

She collapsed into his arms, burying her face in his chest. "It's not fair, Demetrius. It was never fair," She screamed, emotional release in full swing.

"I know, Bunny. I know," His voice was choked, weighed down with the sorrow he held in his heart for her.

Something snapped inside of Bunny like a rubberband. Everything came rushing back to her. She had slipped so far into character, she had almost forgotten what was really happening. Too immersed in the play to stay in touch with reality, Bunny had cracked open, pieces of her spilling out, leaving her exposed.

But it was okay. She was safe. This was her Demetrius, the man who would let no harm come to her outside of what she specifically asked for. She had begged him for this roleplay scenario specifically, laying out her desires methodically. He had finally agreed to it after a waiting period to make sure it was really how she felt.

He picked her back up and took her into the bedroom, setting her down on her feet so he could use the towel to dry her body off. Bunny stood there and let him care for her, still unsure whether her legs could hold out much longer. They didn't have to, however, because he finished quickly and laid her down in the bed, pulling back the sheets to expose the jersey knit set. Her favorite.

"You're all wet," She murmured, running a hand down his shirt. He hummed in response, quickly shedding his shirt and pants and climbing into bed with her.

"Come here, Bunny," He said, pulling her close. She snuggled into his side, putting her head in that cozy spot between his shoulder and neck that she knew so well. She began to cry again. This time it was soft, and he rubbed her back while she let the rest of her emotions flow readily from her cloudy mind

It was easier to feel, be loved, and allow somebody to provide the comfort she craved when she was forced into opening herself. So far in life, she had found no other method that worked quite so well as the domination Demetrius exerted.

She finally quieted, sniffling softly.

"End scene?" He murmured, kissing her forehead.

"Yes, I think so. I think that's all I wanted out of this," She responded quietly, absolutely spent after the days they had played pretend with each other.

"You scared me, y'know that? You got into the role so well, I couldn't tell at some points whether you had lost touch with reality…" Demetrius trailed off, squeezing her until she squeaked.

"I think I might have gotten a little too lost in myself, yeah," She agreed.

After a few moments of silence, Demetrius asked, "Was it everything you wanted?"

"Everything and so much more."

He seemed satisfied with this answer. They

lay there, husband and wife, until they fell asleep nestled into each other.

The next morning, everything was as it was when they weren't playing out a carefully plotted scene. Demetrius woke her with light kisses all over her face as she groaned and weakly pushed him away.

"Good morning, good morning," This sing-song greeting was a daily ritual for them. Bunny, finally switching from stirring to rising, sat up. Her hair was a mess and she felt like her body was falling apart. But that didn't matter. She had never felt lighter in her life.

"Breakfast?" He said, grinning, finally free to ease back into their everyday dynamic. She murmured her agreement and they began dressing for the day.

She had concocted this scenario while researching for school in the furthest reaches of a stuffy, dusty library. Bunny had been hopelessly distracted, trying to figure out how to face the past, how to cope with the trauma, and process the grief she still harbored. And then it hit her.

BDSM had become a way to release the horror inside, to lose control but this time by her own volition. At its core, trauma was a loss of control. It was bad enough to feel that hopelessness as an adult. As a child, truly helpless, she could do nothing to change her circumstances.

But now, she was in the driver's seat.

Demetrius had been the one to introduce her to the scene. It was a way for him to break her down and force her into a position where she could accept his tenderness and love.

He had taught her to take control, and then he had taught her how to let that control go. She couldn't count how many times he had broken her mentally, physically, and spiritually, only to hold her while she fell apart in his arms.

Demetrius was hard and soft and brutish and tender all at the same time. His often dichotomous nature always kept her guessing in the best way possible. She loved him for what he did to her. This time she needed something more.

Once dressed, they made their way arm-in-arm to the kitchen, where Michael stood eating a bagel.

"Oh, is it over?" He said, mouth full of

bread and cream cheese.

"Yeah, we're done," Bunny responded.

"Okay, cool. Anyways, you guys are really fucking weird. Can I leave now?"

"I would prefer it if you did," Demetrius said, still unsure about including his assistant. The man was sleazy enough to do anything for money but was also trustworthy where Demetrius was concerned. They had been best friends since childhood. While Michael was a bit of a fuck-up, he always had Demetrius' back.

"So... I don't get a turn, right?" Michael said hopefully, looking between them.

"Michael, take your money and get the fuck out. For fuck's sake," Bunny groaned. She and Michael had a bit of a history. She had never been his biggest fan, but begrudgingly had learned to love him.

The man threw his hands up, flinging a bit of cream cheese as he did. "Aw, shit," He said, before turning and walking out of the room, thinking better of staying longer to clean it up.

Bunny turned to Demetrius before speaking. "Thank you," She said, entirely caught in his gaze. His gorgeous eyes were like black holes, and she often fell into their event horizon, spinning helplessly into the peaceful nothingness they offered.

"Anything for you, my love. Anything. You know that. Since the day we met, anything," He paused, "But honestly that coffee thing was really fucked up. And trying to break my nose. Oh, and the thing about your parents."

"I was in character," Bunny pouted, sticking out her lower lip and crossing her arms.

"Oh, I know it, honey Bunny," He said the last two words almost as one. It was his favorite nickname for her.

"Well, I know how I can make it up to you," Her eyes were suddenly sultry, and she peeked at him through a half-lidded gaze.

"You're insatiable," Demetrius murmured, corners of his lips lifting.

Without another word, he scooped her up, and carried her back to the bedroom, breakfast forgotten.

Thank You

FOR READING

About the Author

JUNIPER HARTMANN

Juniper Hartmann is a woman in her early 30s from New England. You can just call her Junie if it suits your fancy! Over the past decade, she has worked extensively in the professional writing space.

Her work has been featured across a multitude of websites spanning many industries.

This debut novel is her first foray into the one type of writing she has not yet mastered: creative. She remains anonymous due to the nature of her work. Junie has friends and family.

Also, she kind of enjoys being an enigma.

Junie's Links

SOCIAL & MORE

JuniperHartmann.com

Instagram.com/JuniperHartmann
Tiktok.com/@JuniperHartmann

Acknowledgements

THE BEST PEOPLE

There are too many people to name who helped me discover my ability to write a novel and my passion for doing so. My heart is so full thinking about the massive support I have been shown by everybody in my life.

First and foremost, thank YOU for supporting my journey as an indie author. Buying my book means the world. I cannot adequately express my gratitude.

I absolutely cannot forget my business partner, one of my closest friends who has supported my dream and helped in more ways than I can count. You're a real one!

Finally, my best friend of over 11 years.

You have been my rock through life and none of this would have been possible without you. Thanks for letting me borrow that $50.

THOUGHTS FROM JUNIE

The point of all this is that sometimes not everything is as it seems... and I find that rings true of BDSM relationships. On the surface, they can easily be mistaken for abusive dynamics.

Bunny spends her time running from her trauma and refusing to process it. The inspiration behind the name is two-fold for that reason: she runs from trauma, she runs from him.

Sometimes you must break down into your most basic pieces before you can exercise whatever haunts you. BDSM allows us the ability to break open to another person entirely when done correctly. It is often easier to do so when you are forced (consensually) into it.

Sex is also taboo in our puritanical society. Some people find it easier to be made to act on their sexual desires, taking away their "choice," and therefore blame, in the process.

For Bunny, it is a mixture of all these factors that lead her to pick BDSM as her therapy of choice.

Demetrius is there to pick up the pieces and help her through the aftermath. He does this through meticulous aftercare and keeping a close eye on her throughout each scene.

He gives her what she needs and takes great pride in providing her comfort, love, and a safe place to unload the emotions that surface. When he goes partially soft while watching in the MMFM scene, it happens because he's intent on watching her reactions and ensuring her safety.

It is my hope that you take away from this book a few things: aftercare is king, consent matters most, and BDSM can be an incredible positive when done correctly.

Taylor May

REVIEWER
IG: @READING.WITH.TAYLORRR

"I am 100% confident that **RRR** will have the plot twist of the year for everyone who dives into this journey. You will be stuck in a trance where you forget time it is, what day it is, what your significant other's name is, and ALL the responsibilities you have while reading.

I had my significant other turn the wifi off so I could no longer read… since it was 3:30am and I had to be at work by 7am."

Casey Coffey

REVIEWER
IG: @CUP.OFBOOKS

"Junie hit this one out of the park! Thank you for letting me be an ARC reader of this. I'm gonna need a few days to recover from the book hangover you gave me. Physically I'm here, mentally I'm Bunny in chapter 5."

Chelsea Armstrong

REVIEWER
IG: @CHELSEAREADS2694

"This novel gives you twists and turns.
Closer to the end, I thought it could go one of two
ways and was pleasantly surprised at the outcome.
The writing is phenomenal and the grasp of these
concepts is very educational.

I am still left wanting more of Bunny and
Demetrius' story. Michael is probably my favorite
side character with his quips and I can't wait to
know more about him (hopefully) in the future."

Melanie Egan

R E V I E W E R
IG: @AUSSIEBOOKADDICT

"Hartmann's writing plunges you into a world where danger lurks around every corner, and the stakes are life and death. The intense dynamic between Bunny and her captor keeps readers on the edge of their seats, while the elements of BDSM and banter add layers of complexity to the story.

The fierce, determined Bunny is a compelling protagonist whose journey is both heart-wrenching and empowering."

Samantha Rodriguez

REVIEWER
IG: @THE.BOOKISH.BRUNETTE.483

"Juniper Hartmann did her homework on this one folks. There is a very accurate representation of BDSM and how it can be used to cope with one's mental health.

This book is filled with spicy scenes in graphic detail that leave you hanging onto every word and losing yourself in the story. However, the best thing about this book is the way it ends. This book might as well have slapped me across the face and strutted off."

Ray R·M·

REVIEWER
IG: @RAYRAYSREADS

"WOW! This book sunk its claws into me in the best way possible. When I say I sat down and in an entire evening was engulfed into this amazing story — I mean it. I kicked my feet, I squealed, I giggled, and I gasped.

I was NOT prepared for the twist at the end, nor do I think any of you would be either! It's seductive, it's luscious, it's fucking delicious."

www.ingramcontent.com/pod-product-compliance
Lightning Source LLC
Chambersburg PA
CBHW061536310726
48972CB00008B/2489